The Path of Friendship

Love you so much ♡
Grandma Debbie

The Path of Friendship

of

Friendship

WHAT SHE DIDN'T
REMEMBER

DEBBIE STARK

author
ready

www.authordebbiestark.com

Published by:
Author Ready

Copy Editor: Kim Autrey • Content Editor: Debbie Ihler Rasmussen
Cover design by Ashley Canulli • Haevyn.com
Cover illustation by Larry Stark
Interior book design by Francine Platt, Eden Graphics, Inc.

Paperback ISBN 978-1-958626-22-1
Ebook ISBN 978-1-958626-23-8

Library of Congress Number: 2022921663

Manufactured in the United States of America

First Edition

*Dedicated to
my friends everywhere*

PROLOGUE

....

WE HAVE ALL LOST A FRIEND. Sometimes they move and we lose touch, sometimes they choose a life that no longer includes us. Sadly, sometimes death takes them away.

I lost my best friend of eighteen years, Mayumi.

She didn't move, she didn't die. I didn't lose her in the usual way. I lost her one word at a time.

At first, I barely noticed, and then one day I realized that the Mayumi I knew, the Mayumi I laughed with, talked with, and cried with, was gone. She was replaced by someone I didn't know—someone that didn't know me. It happened right before my eyes.

But what I had that she didn't—was the memory of our friendship.

CHAPTER ONE

....

I HAD NEVER had a Japanese friend. It's not that I was prejudiced or anything, after all, my father was Hispanic, and my mother was German. I just never had the opportunity until me and my husband Paul moved to our new home.

We had lived in the same house for over thirty years. A typical starter home with two bedrooms, one bath, and an unfinished basement. No garage just a carport. We were only married a few months when we bought that house. We worked hard together, making changes to accommodate our family as it grew. We had so many happy years there, but after our kids were raised, my husband and I made the difficult decision to sell our home and move closer to my dad. He was having some health problems, but when he rammed his brand-new Buick through the back of his garage, we knew it was time.

My mother had passed away from cancer, leaving

Dad by himself. He had always been independent, but we knew he couldn't drive any longer.

In the latter part of October, we went house hunting. There was snow on the ground, and it was cold outside.

My friend Gracie was a real estate agent and took us to look for a place closer to my dad. We wanted it to be a good retirement home for us since it would probably be the last house we would ever buy.

We talked about condos and even looked at a few with mixed feelings, but Paul didn't want that. He enjoyed working outside but wanted a smaller yard to putter in.

We were under some pressure as our home was already sold. We had thirty days to find a new place, so the new family could be in before the holidays. We looked at a gray stucco home with stonework below the front room window. More modern than the house we were leaving and within walking distance of my dad's. But we had mixed emotions about the inside.

When we left that house, I saw the house kitty-corner from there had a FOR SALE BY OWNER sign. It was a beige stucco rambler with maroon brick work.

I asked Gracie, "Can we look at that house?"

"Let me go ask," she said and went ahead of us

to see if the owners would let her bring someone through, with no prior notice.

They agreed, and I loved the house! High ceilings, arched doorways, a smaller backyard. It had everything we wanted, but they were asking for more than we had planned on spending.

"Would you be willing to come down on the price?" I asked, but they wouldn't budge.

We left feeling disappointed.

The next couple of houses we looked at didn't compare to that one, and we went back to look at it again and again, finding more things we liked each time. It had a full basement apartment that we didn't need, but Gracie suggested we could always rent it out.

We went home to think about it. I felt bad that if we decided on the house that was FOR SALE BY OWNER, Gracie wouldn't make any commission.

"Be honest, Marcelina, which one do you really want?" asked Paul.

"The more expensive one."

That was all it took. He called the couple and told them that we wanted to buy their house. I then sheepishly called Gracie to tell her I had fallen in love with the house that was "For Sale by Owner."

"Marcelina, don't worry about me. I want you guys to buy the house that you really want." Gracie was such a kind friend, always thinking of others.

We moved into our new house in November. Probably due to the cold and snow, we didn't meet any of our new neighbors that winter. It seemed all we ever saw were garage doors going up and cars backing out. Garage doors going up, cars pulling in. It was like that pretty much the whole winter.

I was always looking trying to see what our new neighbors looked like, but I never did. The neighbor to the east of us kept her blinds closed, except occasionally we would see her peek through a slat. It was so mysterious.

Paul and I loved the brightness of our home, so we kept our blinds open to let the light shine in.

There didn't appear to be any children, and that was okay with us, our kids were grown. Nobody welcomed us to the neighborhood or came over to introduce themselves. Everybody just kept to themselves, and that was fine with us.

The holidays came and went, and by then we were getting tired of winter and staying in the house. So, when spring came, we were anxious to get outside to see what plants were growing.

It was fun to plan the changes we would make to the yard and the flowers we would plant. Paul retired before I did, and he slowly began to meet some of the neighbors when he was out walking our dog, Barkley.

I was still working, so I was getting up at six o'clock am and wouldn't get home from work until 5:30 pm. By then I was too tired to do anything but change my clothes, eat dinner, watch a little TV, and go to bed. Then do it all over again.

On the weekends, I would usually clean the house, never going out much to meet anyone. When our kids were little, we knew all our neighbors. The kids would have sleepovers at each other's houses and play together every day, and we all became good friends and neighbors.

But now that I was middle-aged, I didn't have to neighbor if I didn't feel like it. I just wanted the neighbors to leave us alone. It was Paul who was doing the visiting because he liked to be outside doing yard work. It was then that he met Mayumi and her elderly mother. Mayumi was still working like I was, but her mother was home alone all day, usually gardening out back.

It wasn't until I retired that I first met Mayumi. It seemed very unlikely that we would be close neighbors, let alone close friends. She was a very casual woman. Her black hair was cut in a blunt bob with an inch and a half of graying roots showing. She didn't wear any makeup, and her bronze face was rugged with lines from the sun. She shook my hand, her dry hands felt rough, and her nails were caked with mud from working in her garden. She smiled at me, and I wondered what she thought of this prissy girlie girl that moved next door to her. I was used to dressing up for work and continued to do so, even though I had retired. I always had my hair curled (that was from being a hairdresser when I first married) and put my makeup on every day because I felt very plain without it. I was very conscientious of what I wore, trying hard to disguise the extra ten to fifteen pounds I never got around to losing. I tried hard to keep my appearance up and always remembered a story that my dad had told when I was a teenager living at home.

He said, "Always make sure you look good when you leave the house because you never know who you are going to run into when you're out and about, and what they'll think of you."

Dad went on to tell us he had been working in the yard. Wearing an old pair of khaki shorts covered in paint, a stained white T-shirt, and a sweat-brimmed hat, he ran to a department store to get a tool he needed. He couldn't find what he was looking for and began searching aisle after aisle.

My dad said salespeople would look his way and immediately turn away. No one would help him! That bothered my dad. He said he thought they were thinking *"He's just a dirty Mexican,"* and that made him feel bad. He left the store that day without *ever* receiving any help.

But he didn't stop going to that store, despite the discrimination he felt. He said the next time he went back to the store, he got dressed up first.

He told us, "I wore my Sunday best, even though I don't go to church," and he laughed heartily at his joke. "I wore my light blue dress shirt and a rich-looking tie. I put on a beige vest and shined my shoes to a high gloss. I took your mom with me this time."

Dad was always so proud of our mom; she was attractive, a shapely size seven at best, with highlighted blonde hair. She kept her hair colored because Dad wasn't going to have a wife who looked old. She had her hair done at my salon, and her makeup was expertly applied. That day, she wore tailored brown pants, a beige chiffon blouse, and small gold sandals that clicked as she walked.

They went to that same department store hand in hand and walked down the aisle that my dad had been in the day before. Immediately a salesman approached them.

"Good afternoon, what can I help you folks with today?"

Dad told him what tool he needed. The salesman took him right to it and explained the different brands. He was helpful and attentive. When my dad decided which one he wanted, the salesman walked them to the cash register to check them out.

"Is there anything else I can help you, good folks, with?" he asked.

"That should do it," said my dad.

The salesman said, "Thanks for coming in, we appreciate your business."

My dad never mentioned again the way he had been treated, but that story stayed with me my whole life. I realized that people judge you unfairly by your looks... or was it his race? I was never sure, but my dad's experience would serve me later in my life.

CHAPTER TWO

....

WHEN I RETIRED, I wrote myself a list of things that I wanted to do. I didn't want to sit around and watch daytime TV. I still wanted to feel productive. My retired co-workers told me stories of boredom and not having enough money. I wasn't going to be one of those people.

Little did I know that my saving grace would be to help my Japanese friend who had Alzheimer's. Unbeknownst to her, she helped me.

Mayumi was a small Japanese woman with a good sense of humor, and she loved being outside. She amazed me how she could sit on her haunches for hours weeding, her skin would turn golden brown. I would tease her. "Mayumi, you're getting darker than me, and I'm part Mexican." We would put our arms side by side comparing our olive skin.

I sat out in the heat with her, even though for years I had avoided the sun. I had a good reason. I have a skin disorder called Vitiligo, where pigment is lost in certain areas of the skin, leaving white patches. Being in the sun put me at a higher risk of skin cancer. I never wanted to be tan, it would make the white patches stand out even more.

When I was first diagnosed, I was self-conscious: however, the closer I became to Mayumi, the more time I spent outside. She never made me feel self-conscious about my skin discoloration, and that helped me to accept it. It was a cosmetic thing; it didn't hurt or put me in danger. It was my pride; I had always cared about my looks. But I would hear about friends and family who had life-threatening conditions and decided that I wouldn't trade my affliction for theirs. We would put our folding chairs out in the mornings and have our coffee, and Paul would usually join us. Mayumi would bring doughnuts to share because she knew how much he liked his sweets.

Mayumi taught me a lot about the Japanese community, which I did not know before meeting her. Mayumi's doctor, massage therapist, and dentist were all Japanese. She golfed on a Japanese golf team and was in an all-Japanese bowling league. The friends that she went downtown to see plays with, were all Japanese. Mayumi had told me that she had a toothache one day but couldn't get in to see her dentist. She kept pressing on the tooth to show me where it was hurting.

Finally, I said, "I'll give you the phone number to the office where my daughter works as a dental hygienist, and maybe they can get you in." Even though she was in pain, she wouldn't even consider it. She would wait until she could get into her Japanese dentist.

Mayumi told me that when she was little, the kids would pull their eyes down to a slant and make fun of her. It made her feel so bad. I told her my dad experienced discrimination. He always felt like he had to prove that he was as good as the next guy. He was outgoing and funny and had a great sense of humor, and I think that helped him in life. He was well-liked in the community. Everywhere we kids went, we would meet people who knew our father, and they would rave about what a great guy he was.

"That made us proud," I said, "why was it that one nationality should be better than another? The color of your skin shouldn't matter." Mayumi agreed with me. I didn't experience any discrimination growing up, but my dad had planted those seeds of equality within me.

Today I took Mayumi for a walk. She shared with me that she had been diagnosed with a memory problem (she called it). I wondered what she meant, and weeks later, it was confirmed it was Alzheimer's. Paul and I were very concerned, even though it was the beginning stages of the disease.

I started to notice how Mayumi stumbled around to find a word or a thought. At that time, she was still driving and taking care of herself. Mayumi's mother had passed on, and she now lived alone. I didn't get to know her mother very well because she was always outside in her garden. Occasionally she would sneak over into our backyard, when she knew Paul was out there, tap him on the shoulder nearly scaring him to death, and in her broken English would say, "You want some vegetables?" and she would hand them to him, wrapped in wet newspaper. Some of the Japanese vegetables she gave us, we didn't even know what they were, or how to cook them, but she was always so kind and thoughtful to share what she had in her robust garden. Mayumi missed her mother and was starting to spend more time with Paul and me. Soon after, she and I began taking walks together twice a week.

I was getting closer to Mayumi and started to call her May. She never corrected me; in fact, I think she kind of liked it. During our walks, May would talk about a ninety-year-old aunt that lived in California in an assisted living facility, how she called her every weekend and appeared to be very close with her.

She said it was fun for her to listen to her aunt talk of her old family members that had passed and tell her about the good Japanese food they would make when they all got together.

Those conversations led May to recommend that we try her family's favorite Japanese restaurant.

"We've never tried Japanese food before," I told her. "Only Chinese food. We'll go there, but only if you come with us to help us know what to order."

May agreed to come.

The restaurant was small and authentic, and had partitions around each section for privacy. Japanese pictures with bonsai trees lined the walls. We took our shoes off and sat at a low Horigotatsu table. The recessed floor beneath it allowed our legs to hang down.

May helped us order, and I said, "Don't be ordering me any of that raw fish that you eat. I'm not a fish lover, and besides that, I like my meat cooked!"

I picked up the chopsticks and tried to hold them between my fingers. I dropped them, and we all had a good laugh. So, May showed us how to hold them correctly.

"My family loves coming here to eat. I swear we're here every other week," she said, and she smiled. "My brother knows the owner, and I think because of that, they give my family extra-large portions. I'm glad they do because they always let me take the left-overs home."

Through our conversations with May, we learned about each one of her family members. She had nice things to say about all of them and how thankful she was. She said she didn't know what she would do without her family.

CHAPTER THREE

....

M Y PREVIOUS EXPERIENCE with Alzheimer's was when I worked part-time doing hair at an assisted living/memory care facility near our house. I worked on Fridays and Saturdays and was still working for the State of Utah at that time. In most cases, an adult child would call me to make a hair appointment for their parent who lived at the facility. Usually for a mom who needed a wash and set, or a dad who needed a haircut.

I remember a married couple who lived at the facility together. We visited while I did her hair, and her husband would sit across from us.

When he first sat down, he said, "This is a nice setup you have here."

I thanked him. Then a little later he said it again. "This is a nice setup you have here."

I thanked him again and continued working. He seemed like a mild-mannered man and appeared to have all his faculties together. It was time for me to put his wife under the dryer and give him a haircut.

I said to him, "Okay, it's your turn."

He just sat there. I repeated, "Are you ready for your haircut?"

He didn't budge. Finally, his wife got out from under the dryer and nudged him over to the barber chair to sit down, then she got back under the dryer as if nothing unusual had happened. I put a cape around his shoulders, but he didn't seem to notice. I started to trim his hair, and for the third time he said, "This is a nice setup you have here."

"I like it," I said, and I continued cutting his hair.

The whole time his eyes never left his wife who was still under the dryer reading a magazine. When I finished his haircut, I walked him over to a chair to wait for her.

They were such a cute couple, and I didn't know if they were at the facility because they both had a disability, or if she came to live with him because she needed extra help caring for him.

We talked about their children while I finished her hair.

He interrupted us. "This is a nice setup you have here," but this time he added, "How long have you been here?"

She just smiled at him, and I could see the love

and tenderness they shared. I didn't answer this time. When they left, she held his hand and led him out the door.

The facility had a memory care center on the second floor. It was a lockdown facility for individuals that had advanced stages of Alzheimer's. They had a keypad with a code to get in or out. A daughter of one of those residents asked me to do her mother's hair.

I left the salon and walked down the hall passing rooms where the residents' doors were open. Many were sitting in a chair sleeping while the television played in the background. I wondered why they lived there by themselves, but when I got to the memory care floor, I immediately could see why these individuals had to live here. Some were sitting, staring at nothing; some wandered around aimlessly.

I told the nurse why I was there, and she said, "Beverly is finishing her lunch right now." She walked me to a round table in the kitchen and pointed out Beverly. The CNA was spoon-feeding her.

I introduced myself and told her that her daughter MaryAnn had asked me to do her hair. She didn't even look up at me. I couldn't help but look around the room at the elderly people, some in wheelchairs stuck in front of the TV almost comatose. I had such a weird feeling waiting for them to finish feeding her. I didn't want to appear that I was staring, and I hoped that no one would latch on to me, or even touch me. I was nervous and a little frightened.

This was all new territory for me.

When Beverly finished eating, they led her to the door, telling her as they walked that she was going to have her hair done and how lucky she was. When the CNA punched in the code, a few of the residents hurried to the doorway, wanting to get out. The other CNA softly and politely steered them toward the kitchen for a snack.

I put my arm through hers, we slipped through the doors, and I guided her to the elevator. She seemed out of it and didn't speak at all. Her wild-looking grey hair definitely needed my services.

She did better than I thought she would on the elevator, but when we entered the doorway to the beauty salon, she began to freak out.

I kept saying, "It's ok, MaryAnn wants me to do your hair."

It didn't even faze her.

I tried to lead her over to the barber chair, but she wouldn't move. She looked terrified. When I tried to gently pull her over, she began to scream.

"No!" She didn't say anything else but kept yelling, "No!" and planted her feet firmly on the ground.

She didn't know me, or what was going on, and

she was scared. I wasn't sure what to do next. I didn't know if she would strike me if I continued, but I felt like I had to try to do her hair because the family had paid in advance.

I had never experienced anything like this before. I decided to call upstairs to tell them what was going on, hoping that she wouldn't run away from me. They told me that they would send someone down to get her.

I got her to sit down, and close to her ear, I softly said, "They're coming to get you, it's okay." That seemed to calm her, but her flat eyes stared straight ahead.

I didn't dare touch her. I don't know if she thought it was her daughter MaryAnn or who, but she stayed there waiting. She didn't contest being led back by the young CNA that came to get her.

I decided after working with that population of individuals, I wanted to keep doing something positive for them, by doing their hair and showing kindness to each person. That night, I told Paul about my day at the beauty salon, and how many people I dealt with at the facility who had memory problems.

"It was so sad, Paul, to see all those folks whose lives had been completely turned upside down from their normal way of living, and they can't do a damn thing about it."

Some residents were worse than others. It could be very challenging. After talking to the nurse on staff, I slowly began to recognize the different stages of Alzheimer's. Those individuals that lived on the first floor had confusion and an inability to gauge time but were not a danger to themselves or anyone else. They were free to roam where they wanted, sometimes just coming into the salon to visit, or would just sit and watch. The individual's upstairs on the second floor required twenty-four-hour care. Some of them had mood swings and would be violent at times and had to be sedated. Other residents had no memory of who they were or where they were.

One red-haired lady that lived on the first floor would slip in while I was working. She never said a word but would sit and watch.

One day she surprised me. "What time are you doing my hair?"

"You don't have an appointment that I am aware of, or did your family call?"

She didn't answer but stood to leave. She stopped and asked, "Where do I go to eat dinner?"

I was at a point where I could stop for a few seconds, so I walked out into the hall with her and pointed toward the receptionist's desk. "She'll show you."

The next morning, I got a call from someone in that same woman's family asking me to color her hair. She came on her own and was there at the right time. I noticed she was wearing ruby earrings in her pierced ears. She had gold bracelets on both arms and a gold crucifix around her neck. I brushed her hair out and mixed her color.

"Do you want to take your jewelry off before I apply your hair color?"

She said no, so I went ahead with it.

While she waited the forty-five minutes to process, I fit in a quick hair cut for a lady in a wheelchair.

"Good morning," I said, as she wheeled her way across the floor.

"I can't get my neck back in that chair," she said in her squeaky voice. "You'll have to let me stay in my wheelchair to do my hair."

I was caught a little off guard because I knew that she would be too low to reach the wash basin.

Then she added, "The other hairdresser that worked here, let me stay in my wheelchair, and just pushed me up to the sink."

I wanted to accommodate her the best that I could, so I moved the barber chair out of the way so that she could back up to the shampoo bowl. It was hard getting her short neck back into the sink, and I ended up soaking her. The water ran down her back, even reaching her underwear. She was furious with me, yelling in that irritating voice that reminded me of

Fran Drescher, who played in the sitcom *The Nanny*.

I apologized and told her that I couldn't get her back far enough without getting her out of her wheelchair. After I cut her hair, I held the blow dryer on her back, trying to slightly dry her clothes and make things right with her. She felt a little better, paid me, and rolled away.

The red head didn't say a word even though she had witnessed the whole fiasco. It was time for me to wash the coloring out of her hair. I cut and styled her hair and then led her to the door and asked her, "Do you know how to find your room?"

The blank look on her face told me she couldn't. No wonder, everybody's doors looked the same, except for those that chose to hang something on the front to distinguish it from the others.

Just then a CNA was passing and said, "Hilda, you look so nice! Can I show you to your room?"

When I was cleaning out the wash basin, I noticed a ruby earring in the basket of the sink. I picked it out and immediately knew that it was Hilda's, the red-headed lady. I knew I should have insisted that she take them out, but I was afraid she would lose them. I was so grateful that it hadn't gone down the drain. I set it aside and started gathering up the dirty towels. I swept and mopped the floor and wiped everything down. I picked up the basket of dirty towels and my purse and left, never remembering the ruby earring. The shop was closed and locked until Tuesday when the other hairdresser worked.

I was getting ready for my full-time job when I put my pierced earrings in, and I suddenly remembered the ruby earring that I had set on the side of the sink.

"Damn," I said out loud. It was too early to call the salon because they didn't open until ten o'clock. I made myself a reminder to call as soon as they opened. I wondered if Hilda would have even noticed that she was missing an earring, or even remembered.

I went to work and got busy making phone calls and attending a team meeting. I came back to my office to get my coffee cup when I saw my reminder note to call the salon at the memory care facility. I called the shop, and Sheila answered. "Did you happen to see a ruby earring on the side of the sink?"

She hesitated, "No, I don't see it."

I immediately felt my anxiety kick in because I knew it was there when I left. The shop had been locked, and nobody else could have gotten in. I wondered if Sheila had pocketed the ruby earring knowing perhaps that the person that owned it wouldn't remember that it was missing.

I asked Sheila to report it to the front desk lost and found thinking it would never show up now.

Then I got nervous, *I hope they don't think I would keep it. I would never do such a thing.*

I had asked Sheila to call me back if she found it, but I didn't hear from her that entire week. What would someone want with a single earring? It couldn't be the cleaning staff because we did our cleaning. When I arrived the next Friday morning, there was an envelope with my name on it. I opened it up, and there was a note and the ruby earring. The note was from Sheila. She said she found the earring on the floor. Really? I had mopped the floor that night before I went home and knew it wasn't there. I knew it was on the side of the sink. I wondered if she was going to keep it and then had a change of heart, afraid that she would be found out. I didn't know.

As usual that next Friday, Hilda wandered in. She didn't say anything about her missing earring but had a different pair on. They were beautiful diamond studs. I decided to ask, "Are you missing a ruby earring?"

She looked puzzled. I knew the earring was hers. My next client came in, and I handed Hilda the envelope with her earring inside and told her to take it back to her room and put it where it would be safe with its match. She took it from me and left.

I really liked doing hair at the assisted living center, but it was hard work. A lot of the people needed physical assistance, and it was taxing on my back. The extra money I made was nice, but more than anything, it made me feel good to do something for these folks who needed me. I was always tired when I got home from the shop on Friday and Saturday evenings. I never wanted to go out anymore. I just wanted Paul to go get takeout while I showered and put my pajamas on. I really didn't want to quit, but I didn't want it to cause problems between Paul and me either. I just knew it was hard on me physically as well as emotionally.

I grew very fond of the residents who lived there. I had gotten so used to being around people with Alzheimer's and other disabilities that I wasn't afraid or uncomfortable any longer. I knew by now, that they had their good days and their bad days. Sometimes they conversed, and other times they were in their little world. I was surprised one Saturday when Hilda wandered in and asked me if I would like to have dinner with her in the dining room when I got off.

"That's so nice of you to ask me, Hilda, it really is, but I need to get home to my husband, I've been gone all day."

I felt bad saying that to her. She didn't have a husband to go home to. I looked at her sad face, surprised she had even spoken to me, let alone invited me to dinner. She never really talked to anyone.

I decided to call Paul and tell him that I was going to join Hilda for dinner and that I couldn't stand the disappointment on her face. I told him I would be home later and would stop and pick a burger up for him to have for his dinner.

Hilda waited patiently for me to finish up my last patron. I took my apron off and escorted her to the dining hall. She surprised me by slipping her arm through mine as we walked, and I noticed that everyone was staring at us as we entered the room.

I said hello to the individuals I recognized from the salon. Others probably wondered what I was doing with Hilda, the woman who was always lost and rarely spoke. We sat down at a table by ourselves, and the server asked us what we would like to drink.

I said, "A Diet Coke please," but Hilda never answered.

The server walked away, and when she came back, she had my Diet Coke and set a cup of coffee with cream in front of Hilda. I thought I detected a slight smile on her lips as she took a drink of the hot coffee.

We weren't asked what we wanted to eat; instead, the server brought out two plates with roast beef and mashed potatoes, gravy, and green beans. It was a bland dinner, and Hilda just sat there watching me. It wasn't until I scooped up a forkful of potatoes that she did the same. She never looked me in the eyes and would only take a bite if I would.

I tried to talk to her, but she wouldn't say anything, only mimicking what I would do. One of the snooty residents came over to our table and said, "It's nice that you could stay for dinner."

She thinks I'm looking for a free meal.

"Yes, Hilda invited me to join her."

Her eyebrows raised, and she looked surprised. Everyone knew Hilda didn't communicate often with other people. Whether anybody believed that Hilda spoke to me that day didn't matter to me. I knew she had. Was it a thank-you gesture for finding her ruby earring? I didn't know, but I sort of thought it was.

I worked at the facility for over a year and a half. It wasn't easy working two jobs, but I felt good about what I was doing. I was helping those individuals feel good about themselves, and in turn, that made me feel good.

CHAPTER FOUR

ONE DAY I invited May to go to the farmer's market with me the next Saturday morning.

She said she would love to go.

I told her I would pick her up at ten o'clock and suggested she bring a bag for her vegetables and fruit. I also told her not to eat breakfast because we would get a breakfast tamale from one of the food trucks.

"I can't wait," she said. "That's the only place I've ever had them."

"Me too. They sell out every time the food truck is there." I went home anticipating our outing together.

The next morning, I pulled into May's driveway and honked. I waited for five minutes and honked again. She still didn't come out, so I shut off my engine, walked up to her door, and rang the doorbell.

No answer. I knew how much May liked going to the farmer's market, so I was surprised that she would forget. I walked around to the backyard to see if she was there. There she was hands covered in mud and dirt. She looked at me as though I was an intruder.

She seriously didn't remember.

"Did you forget that we were going to the farmer's market today?"

She looked stumped. She wasn't ready. In fact, she was weeding her backyard.

I could tell that she was embarrassed. I told her it was okay and suggested we try the next week.

Later when I mentioned it to her family, they said that she had forgotten other appointments as well. I decided that I would buy her a large calendar to hang on her fridge, so she could write down her appointments, and it would be in full view.

"Thank you so much, Marcelina," she said. "How much do I owe you for it?"

"Nothing. I think you'll really like having this to put your appointments on."

She never did hang the calendar. Much later I saw it stashed behind a kitchen chair, blank as the day I gave it to her.

Betty lived across the street from May. She called me one day. "Hey, Marcelina, I know that you're close to May, and sometimes you talk to her family. The other day, Jake and I were behind her car as she was pulling out of our subdivision. We noticed how slow she was driving, and how unsure she seemed of when to turn left. She waited so long that eventually she was stuck out in the middle of the intersection when the light turned, almost causing an accident. I know you told me that she has Alzheimer's, and I just wondered if it's safe for her to still be driving."

I told Betty that May told me she tried to drive to the grocery store and got lost on several occasions but didn't want her family to know. I also noticed that she had some scratches and dents on her car that weren't there before.

"Thanks for your concern, Betty, you're a good neighbor. I'll call May's brother."

I explained to May's brother the neighbors cared about Mayumi and didn't want her to get hurt, or for that matter, hurt anyone else. He knew what I was talking about. Her memory was getting worse. He just didn't know how he was going to take her keys away. He knew that she would be devastated. She had always been so self-sufficient and was proud of it.

The next day, May got ready to leave to go meet some of her friends for lunch. She got in her car to start it, and it wouldn't start. She tried and tried and finally came over to see if Paul would look at it for her. He followed her over to the garage where her car was parked and tried to start it, but it wouldn't turn over.

He said, "I think you might have a dead battery, May. Do you have any jumpers? I lent mine to my son, and he never gave them back."

May looked in the pile of junk that was stacked to the side of the car and said, "I know I had some at one time." She was getting flustered.

I finally said, "Can't you just call one of your friends to pick you up? Tell them you're having car problems?" I knew she hated to depend on other people.

Then I said, "I know, I'll run you over, and one of them can bring you back, how's that?"

She looked relieved. "Ok, thanks so much, Marcelina, I really appreciate you."

Later that evening, she told me she called her brother to tell him about her car. He said he would look into her car problem, but never did. Paul and I thought he might have come over early in the morning, or late at night, and disconnected her battery, so she couldn't drive anymore. Every time she reminded him about it, he would say the same thing, "We'll look into it, Sis. I can take you wherever you need to go."

Months went by with her car out of commission. She would threaten she was going to call AAA to come and fix her car. She was mad that her brother was putting her off. She even threatened to walk to a car repair shop to ask them to come and tow it. It was located east of our subdivision and way too far for her to walk. I never offered to take her, knowing it was her brother's way of keeping her from driving, for her own good.

I asked May if she wanted to go to the nail shop with me to have a pedicure, and she accepted, saying she was glad to get out of the house. The salon I go to wasn't very busy that day. Anna, the manager, had the door propped open, so the nice breeze could filter into the salon.

I liked going to this particular nail salon because they were always so friendly. They greeted me by name and handed me a bottle of water. If you chose to converse, the nail tech would talk to you.

On the other hand, I used this time to relax, almost meditate. I would close my eyes. I had confidence that she didn't need me to watch what she was doing. Today Anna had Vietnamese music softly playing in the background. She had hired a new nail tech who was Vietnamese like they all were, and they would talk to each other in their native language.

At times when they laughed, I wondered if they were talking about us. They worked very fast but never made me feel rushed.

The nail tech asked May, "What nationality are you?" May was quick to let her know. "I'm Japanese," and quickly added, almost defensively, "but I was born in the United States."

They needed extra time on May's feet because hers were in such bad shape. They were cracked and dry from working in the dirt in her flip-flops. She watched their every move and refused when they offered to turn the back massager on for her. She was mad that they had asked her what nationality she was. Later, she said, "I didn't ask them what nationality they were."

She was offended and complained afterward that they were rough on her feet and that the color they put on her was too bright.

I told her they probably had to scrub hard to get the callouses off her heels. From my experience, they went out of their way to make their customers happy. May was just having one of those days.

"Didn't they ask you what color you wanted?"

"Yes," she said, "but it looked different in the bottle."

I felt a little protective of the salon. "Well, that wasn't their fault."

I decided on the way home that I wasn't going to ask her to go with me ever again. That was a special treat to myself, and I didn't want her to ruin it for me. I loved Anna's nail shop.

I could feel myself getting upset with her. I just

thought she would appreciate getting out and being pampered. Maybe she was just grumpy that day. I didn't know what was going on in that head of hers. I'm sure she was frustrated at not being able to do things for herself.

After I thought about how hard it must be, I decided to cut her some slack. To not be able to jump in her car and go somewhere, anywhere, would be so hard. I decided to try to be more understanding.

On the way home, I asked her, "Do you like Mexican food?"

"Oh yes," she said.

"How would you like to try a Mexican restaurant my dad used to like to go to when he was alive?"

She perked up. "I would love to."

When we were eating, she seemed better, not as edgy. Of course, food always made her happy, she loved to eat. We talked about how both of our dads were smokers when we were young and lived at our parents' homes. We shared that we had concerns about secondhand smoke and our chances of getting cancer. I told her that my mother never drove when we were kids.

"My mom didn't drive either." She seemed excited we had that in common.

We talked about how our mothers would load us on the city bus to go downtown to go school shopping, and how much fun it was. I was surprised at how similar our lives were, and I'm sure she was too. We certainly didn't *look* the same, but we soon found that we were more alike than different.

After years of walking together, I decided to take May down the street where my dad used to live. We stood in front of the house where I grew up. I told her when the subdivision was new, there weren't any trees behind my house. There was a drive-in movie across the street, and my sister and I would sleep out with the neighbor girls in our backyard. When all the cars would turn up the outdoor speakers that would hang on their car door windows, we could hear the movie.

The people that bought my parents' house took pride in it, and that made me feel good for May to see it looking so nice.

"My parents worked together in the yard after they retired. They loved planting flowers and keeping their yard trimmed, pretty much like Paul and I do."

May said, "My mother always loved to work in her vegetable garden."

When her kids were small, their mom worked for a Japanese family in their large garden. She told me that she would take her kids along, and they played while their mother worked in the hot sun. She said that later in life, her mother worked in the school lunch department at the high school we had both attended. I thought about the differences between our parents, and how we were raised. The universal thing about our two families was love.

When I got home, I pulled out my yearbook and turned to the page that had the lunch workers' pictures. There she was, a Japanese lady with a hairnet covering her black hair. I knew it was her mother, May had her smile. I called her to tell her I found her mom's picture.

The next day, I heard a tap, tap, tap on the storm door, May's signature knock. She wanted to see the picture of her mother in my yearbook. Her mother had been gone for years now, and May missed her terribly. I enjoyed listening to her talk about her mom, and how her Japanese friends would gather together, each bringing a delectable dish they had cooked. May wished she could remember the recipes that they had shared with her back then, but she couldn't.

Often, we talked about how both of us had so many pictures of our families.

"I have piles of pictures that need to be put into a scrapbook, and I never seem to have time to do it."

"I know what you mean," May said. "I have tons of pictures from Japan that I need to put in a photo album as well."

"Next time we go to the craft store, let's pick up scrapbooks and photo albums for both of us, and I'll help you put them together."

I knew she wouldn't be able to do it on her own.

CHAPTER FIVE

. . . .

ᴇARLY ON IN OUR FRIENDSHIP when I talked to my other friends about May, I would say, "You know my Japanese friend that lives next door to me?" And then tell them about a fun day or the funny things she would say or do. It was my way of explaining which neighbor I was talking about.

When I first met her and talked about her, we would say there is this Japanese lady that lives on the east side of us and so on. She became a constant conversation when my married kids came over for dinners on Sundays. They could tell how fond their dad and I were of her. We told our kids and our friends that May had been diagnosed with Alzheimer's, and how sick we felt about it. We could now see how it was affecting her in so many ways. The first thing our kids wanted to know was, "Who will take care of her when she gets bad?"

"I guess her family will," was all we said.

On one of our walks down to the park, I talked about our friends, Jackie and Talon, who Paul and I did all our traveling with, and how much fun we had together.

I told her we were going to fly to Las Vegas to see them and stay at their second home.

"We got tickets to see the Eagles Live, I'm so excited. I've always wanted to see them, but I've only seen The Tribute band that played at our State Fair. They were really good, May, but this will be the real thing. I can't wait to go! The only drawback is, I really don't like to fly, it gives me anxiety."

May said, "Oh I love to fly. From Salt Lake to Tokyo takes about thirteen hours and fifty-four minutes, and I love every minute of it."

I was surprised that she remembered that. I asked her what cities she had been to in Japan since she had been there four times already, but she couldn't remember the names except for Tokyo. She told me that she was going to go there again, with her cousins this time.

I told her that even though I didn't like to fly, I would continue to travel but had to take lorazepam to calm my nerves. Las Vegas would be a short flight, and I was excited to spend time with our friends since we hadn't seen them in months.

"How long are you going for?" she asked.

"Three nights and four days."

She always wanted to know what we were doing with our dog while we were gone. I told her that our son and his family were going to take him to their house.

When our trip came up a couple of weeks later, May acted sulky. She was like that anytime we were going away.

But I didn't let that stop me from being excited to go. The next morning as we loaded our bags into the back of my Ford escape, May was out on her front lawn watching us. I know she probably felt bad because we're getting away, and she's stuck at home.

When the last bag was put in the car I said, "Goodbye, May."

"Bye," she said quickly and turned away.

While we were waiting at the airport, I mentioned to Paul how sulky May seemed that we were going on a vacation.

"Well don't tell her when we're going away anymore."

"She seems to keep track of everything we do."

He put his arm around me and leaned in. "Let's not talk about May anymore, okay? Let's just enjoy our time away."

We boarded the plane, and I instantly felt anxious. I had forgotten to take my lorazepam, and I felt nervous and a little shaky.

Hoping to be distracted, I watched people stuff their bags into the overhead storage compartments, even though there was very little room. I felt like I needed to go to the bathroom, and I knew it was because of the anxiety I was feeling. But I really didn't want to work my way back through the people in the aisles since we were seated in the middle section of the row.

Soon we were all in our seats when the flight attendant gave her preflight emergency instructions. All it did was make me more nervous. I picked up a magazine and began thumbing through it, not really concentrating. The light came on to tell us to buckle our seatbelts, we were getting ready for takeoff. I could feel my heart beating in my chest. I hated that thrust of power that pushed you into the back of your seat as the plane climbed high into the air.

I closed my eyes and pictured May telling me in her soft voice, how short this plane ride to Las Vegas was going to be, and how she loved flying and was never scared. I pictured her smiley face talking about the places she had flown to that were so far away, and she had never encountered any problems. I started to settle down.

It wasn't long before the flight attendant was coming around to see who wanted drinks. I told Paul to order me a rum and Coke while I went to the bathroom, even though the urge had subsided.

As I passed row after row, I wondered if they were all going to Las Vegas like us, or if there was a layover, and they were on their way to other places. When I came back to our seats, our drinks had come. I drank my rum and Coke and started to feel a little calmer.

We landed without much ado. Our friends Jackie and Talon picked us up at the crowded airport, and we hopped on the freeway to the gridlock of the Las Vegas traffic welcoming us. I looked out to see the casinos in the distance. The Luxor with its pyramid shape was visible, and I found that I was cranking my neck as we passed to try and see the other casinos that were in view. I couldn't wait to see them all lit up at night. Those neon signs drew you in. I could see why it was nicknamed *the* City of Lights.

We had been to Las Vegas before, but we still always felt the excitement of walking down the strip in the evening sipping a margarita as we strolled shoulder to shoulder with the other tourists. When we arrived at Talon and Jackie's house, we pulled into their over-55 community just off Flamingo Way. Our friends always made us feel so welcome, even though they were constantly having people visit them because of living in Las Vegas. Jackie and Talon weren't gamblers, but they enjoyed the warm weather, especially when it was winter in Salt Lake.

We usually went to visit them in October when it was starting to cool down in Utah.

One year we went over the Thanksgiving holiday, trying to give ourselves a break from the work of fixing the whole spread of a Thanksgiving meal. Turkey, dressing, mashed potatoes and gravy, sweet potatoes, and of course, we would have made homemade rolls and pies. It was all very tiring. Sometimes, we were too tired from the preparation to even enjoy the meal. We always cooked as a team in our house. Paul was the better cook of the two of us, but I was always at his side helping. We wondered if our kids even realized how much work it was for us to fix that meal. We knew the day would come when they would find out for themselves what went into it.

The only problem was that year in Las Vegas didn't even seem like Thanksgiving. The casinos were just as packed with people as at any other time.

The Thanksgiving meal was okay but not like what we would have had at home, and I missed my kids and grandkids. It was weird that we were not together on a holiday. I told Paul "I don't want to ever be gone on a holiday again, no matter how much work it is, okay?"

This year's trip to Las Vegas was different. We had never been to Sin City in the summertime, but we wanted to see the Eagles so bad that we decided to make the trip. The sweltering heat was almost more than we could endure as we walked down the strip guzzling our water bottles. Jackie suggested we get out of the heat and pop into the Mirage to take a break.

Paul wandered over to the roulette table, and I walked away not wanting to jinx him. I thought about playing a game of twenty-one, but knew I was too much of an amateur and decided to play the slot machines instead. After being in there for a couple of hours, the cigarette smoke was starting to get to me, and I didn't want to waste any more money. I'm sure our friends had had enough, so we left, went back to their house, put some oldies music on, and played cards. It was nice to visit and laugh and talk about the past trips that we had gone on, and the things that we liked best about each trip. It was getting late, and we decided we better go to bed since we knew we would be out late the next night for our concert. We said goodnight to Jackie and Talon and went to bed.

That night I was in a deep sleep when my cell phone rang. It startled us both.

Oh no! Hopefully, this is not one of our kids.

I jumped out of bed and grabbed my phone off the dresser.

"Hello?"

No one was there. I waited to see if there was a delayed response, I could only hear breathing.

I said hello again and waited. Nothing, so I hung up, put it back on the dresser, and climbed back into bed. I was relieved that nothing was wrong at home. Paul didn't ask me about the call, but I had just crawled back in bed and snuggled up next to him when the damn thing rang again.

I hurried so fast this time, not wanting the noise to wake our friends, that I stubbed my toe before I was able to say hello.

"Shit!" A few seconds of silence went by, and I angrily asked, "Who is this?"

"Marcelina?" May said softly.

"May, is that you?"

"Someone called me and hung up."

"I didn't call you, you called me and hung up. It's two o'clock in the morning. May, you shouldn't be calling anyone this late."

"Where are you?"

I was so irritated at her for bothering us, and I knew she could hear it in my voice, but I couldn't help it. "You need to go back to bed, and I'll call you in the morning."

I didn't call her as I promised, and she left us alone for the rest of our trip.

The night of our Eagles concert was so much fun.

We had reservations for dinner at a steakhouse. Our table was covered in a white linen tablecloth with matching linen napkins. There was a dimly lit votive candle in a crystal holder in the middle of the table. The restaurant was elegant, and we felt like royalty. We ordered a bottle of red wine and steaks for all of us. When our waiter came around and asked if we wanted dessert, we all groaned, "We're too full." We finished the last of our wine. The guys paid the bill, and we left for our concert.

As the concert neared the end, I felt so tired. Between the cocktails, the heavy meal, and the physical activity of dancing, I was feeling my age. I could tell Paul was too because he yawned, and that made Jackie yawn.

We were all feeling our age.

The Eagles were about to play their last greatest hit, "Desperado." Everybody was on their feet. We sang along with the band, and I felt Paul lean into me to give me a peck on the cheek. We danced to this song so many times in our life. We had quite the night. It had been a very special evening. The four of us talked all the way home about how good the band sounded. We were glad we went.

The next day we slept late. There was no reason for us to get up early. At home, Paul was an early riser to take our dog out to go potty, but this morning he was off duty, and he deserved that after eight long years. It was nice to have friends we got along with and felt comfortable staying with. We all had friends who after many years ended up getting a divorce. Both our marriages were rock solid. Someone asked me one time what was the secret of being married for so long, and I said, "Respect, you had to have respect for one another."

No midlife crisis in our marriage, thank goodness. No infidelity. We were kind to one another, and that was an important trait in our marriage.

That morning our friends drove us to Lake Mead Marina which was about half an hour's drive from their house. We sat out in their outside dining area that was at the edge of the lake, where various kinds of boats were docked. It was a perfect temperature, and we had a great view of the water. The seagulls came right up to our table looking for something to eat.

We ordered lunch and could have stayed there all day, lazily watching the colorful sailboats. It felt so relaxing to be able to sit out there and not have to think about May and how she was doing.

We were so glad to be on a vacation with our friends. We talked more about the concert, how it was a sellout, every seat was filled, and how the excitement of the crowd can make a difference in how fun a concert is.

"I couldn't believe how there were people of all ages there, young and old," I said. "I was so tired by the end of the concert; I can tell we're getting older."

"I know, we were tired too," said Jackie.

Then Talon reminded us of a concert we went to in Deer Valley and how we sat outside on blankets, and the whole hillside was covered with people who had come to see Crosby, Stills & Nash.

So many years, and such good friends. I didn't want to think about when one of us goes, even though we were getting on in life. We all wanted to make the best of our lives, while we could.

After an amazing trip, we made it home and picked up Barkley. I wondered if May would be mad at me for not calling her back, but more likely she wouldn't even remember calling.

CHAPTER SIX

······················

THE NEXT WEEK, we were back at the park to do our walking. After a couple of years, we were now walking five days a week. Two baseball games were going on. It reminded me of when I was a young girl, and the church I belonged to provided a variety of activities for my sisters and me to be involved in. Our dad played men's softball, and he was a good player, even though his forte was football when he was in high school. I remembered going to his games with our mom and watching him. He enjoyed it and loved having us there to support him.

When I tell my grandkids about the activities that I used to be involved in, they don't seem to be too impressed. Nowadays, they play video games or lay on their beds staring at their iPhones for hours.

I said to May, "Kids don't even seem to want to go outside and play anymore. Paul talks about when he was young, he would ride his bike with his friends clear out to the airport to watch the planes land. He was usually gone all day, and his mom didn't even worry about him because she knew he would be home for dinner."

I chuckled, and May said, "I know what you're talking about, playing sports. I played all kinds of sports when I was young. I played softball, tennis, and golf, and I bowled. I was very active."

It seemed she felt sad that she wasn't able to do that any longer.

May loved going to the senior center and making origami. Folding pieces of paper into shapes, which was associated with her Japanese culture. She liked to have lunch there because they served salmon on Tuesdays. She would always tell me about the people who she sat with to eat her lunch. They would talk for hours, and I almost felt like I knew these people. She always invited me to join her, but I felt like I was too young to go to a Senior Center (at least I told myself that).

When May couldn't drive herself to go anymore, I offered to take her once a week and pick her up because she would tell me how much she missed going but didn't want to be a burden to anyone to ask for a ride.

She said, "I don't need to go anymore."

"May, you enjoy that, you need to get out. It's

good for you to interact with other people."

I insisted I was going to take her and pick her up once a week. That next Tuesday, I dropped her off at the Senior Center and told her to have fun and that I would be back later to pick her up. She had been there for three hours like we had decided on, so I drove back to the center, but she wasn't out front like she was supposed to be. I waited and kept my car running because it was hot outside, and I needed the air conditioning on.

I waited and waited. I kept looking at the large glass windows to see if I could see her. I was getting impatient, so I decided to shut my engine off and go inside. I was stopped at the receptionist's desk, where they asked me if I wanted to join.

"No thank you. I'm actually here to pick up Mayumi, do you know her?"

"Oh yes, we know Mayumi, she's in the lunchroom," and she pointed down the hall.

I went into the large room that was filled with round tables. There were people at almost every table. I saw May seated at a table of only Japanese people. I think I was so surprised because all this time I had listened to her talk about her friends at the Senior Center, I pictured them as Caucasian. I never really thought about them being Japanese.

May looked up and saw me. "Do you want to sit

down and have dessert with us? They have cake and coffee."

She introduced me to her friends. "This is my good neighbor, Marcelina."

Everyone smiled and acted as if they were familiar with me already.

The lady next to May said, "So you're the neighbor that's so good to her, she always talks about you."

May beamed. They made me feel really welcome. One of the ladies said, "It's so nice of you to bring Mayumi to the center and pick her up."

"Of course, I love her. We're really good friends."

They started talking about a class they had gone to that day, and I looked around at the other tables. The Caucasian people were seated at a table laughing and talking just like May's table was. I walked over to get myself a cup of coffee to go with my cake, and as I looked further away, I saw a table of Hispanic people all sitting together playing cards and having a good time as well. I wondered; is this the way it is here? Each race staying within their kind? Segregation? Really? It's 2021, people! Was it because they were seniors? I would never think about not sitting with May's friends. I never thought about people's ethnicity. I loved that our neighborhood was so diverse. I never thought twice about the color of someone's skin. I always loved to hear people speak who had accents but usually couldn't guess where they were from.

One of our favorite neighbors that lived kitty-corner from us was Indian. The wife was born in India. We loved their family. Their black-haired boys had the darkest brown eyes, and we loved to watch them play basketball in their front yard. Next door to us, the neighbors had a gay pride flag hanging in their window. The neighbors across the street had a sign in their yard saying Black Lives Matter, which we liked. I was glad that our neighbors all accepted each other. It wasn't as if we were best friends with everybody as I had become with May, but you could always expect a hello or a hand wave when you went by. We had Chinese, Japanese, Indian, and Afghan neighbors, and me who was half-Hispanic. Black, white, whatever, we all watched out for one another. We had such fun block parties where we could all be together and visit.

I liked where we lived, and so did May. She never felt different than anyone else.

I don't know why I felt like it was my job to take care of May, after all, she had a family. But I did. I always offered to take her grocery shopping. She never made a list of what she needed. She almost wandered around aimlessly now. I would watch her with concern and would reel her back in.

"Do you need cereal?"

She would hesitate. "Oh yes," but would stare at the cereals and not be able to pick one out.

I would choose one for her. "This is what Paul and I like; do you want to try it?" She would always go along with it. I think the grocery store was so overwhelming to her, yet she liked to go. When I told her about how she could order her groceries online and have them delivered, she was quick to say no.

I didn't know if she said no because she thought she couldn't do it, or because she enjoyed going with me. I always tried to suggest things that I thought would be easy for her, since her family didn't want her to use the stove anymore. I would lead her around the whole store trying to think of necessities she wouldn't remember to get. She always went to the sushi counter to say hello to the Asian man there. She would smile a big smile when she saw him as if they were best friends. I didn't know much about sushi because I don't eat it, but thankfully the Asian man seemed to know he needed to assist her in her selections.

I then took her over to the cold case where they had pre-made meals that could be warmed up in the microwave. I thought those would be good for her, and she bought three of them.

Our last stop was at the bakery. May loved to buy

doughnuts. She always asked me, "Which one will Paul like?"

"Anything with nuts."

She would get two for him, and then ask me, "What kind do you want?"

"Don't get any for me, I'm diabetic, I shouldn't have any." I would usually break down and end up having one with May and Paul anyway. When we came home from grocery shopping, I would help her unpack the back of my car with both of our groceries, having to sort out what was hers, and what was mine. I never really got everything that I needed at the store because I was always too concerned about getting what she needed. She would have me load her groceries on her front porch, not letting me in her house. That was okay. I was just glad she had food, and I didn't have to worry about her for a while.

May loved to eat. Her whole face would light up when the food tasted good to her. Whenever we would make a pot of chili or large amounts of soups or my famous *Million Dollar Spaghetti*, we always shared with her.

The day after we had taken her some dinner, I would ask her, "How did you like your dinner that we brought over to you last night?"

She would smile that big smile, showing her small, crooked teeth. "It was good."

If we didn't take food over to her, we would take her out with us for fast food. It was fun to take someone out who was appreciative. It made it more enjoyable. Paul had that in common with her. He loved to eat, and because he was so active, he never seemed to worry about what he ate. May was little and could eat whatever she wanted as well. I, on the other hand, always fought to keep my weight down.

CHAPTER SEVEN

....

*B*EFORE MAY had her memory problem and was still employed, she worked hard at her job and would stay late, sometimes not getting home until after dark. She said that her mother would worry about her being out late. May told me that she really liked the owner of the company. He was an older gentleman, and he liked her as well and appreciated her dedication.

One year, he surprised her by giving her a diamond tennis bracelet after working so many years for him. He was so personable and made her feel glad to be a part of the team. He told her that he was taking care of his wife who had cancer and was thinking of retiring. She hated to hear that since he was so good to her. His company made parts for a Utah gun manufacturer, and the day before he retired, he gave her a pearled-handled handgun. She knew she would never use the gun, but it was a beautiful piece, and she felt very nostalgic about him giving it to her.

After he retired, things changed for May. His sons took over running the company.

May said to me, "They don't treat me very well. They aren't like their father at all. They told me that I talk too much to the girls in the office."

She knew that wasn't true. She had always gone above and beyond what was expected of her. She was totally dedicated to her job, but the sons failed to see that. They started making it hard for her to take any time off to go to her medical appointments. They started looking over her shoulder, micromanaging her. She hated that feeling.

She said, "I can tell that they don't like me."

It's true. Her memory was declining now, and mistakes were being made, and they would call her on it. She started to have to work even harder to make things right. They were being so mean to her. She asked her Hispanic coworker if she had noticed the different treatment between the father that owned the company and his sons that were running it now. The truth was, the employees did notice how hard they were being on May but didn't dare speak up, for fear of losing their jobs.

She wasn't aware of the decline in her work skills, but she did know it took her longer to get the payroll out. She stopped going to Einstein's to pick up bagels in the morning for the girls in the office. She turned down all offers to go to lunch with them; instead, she would work straight through.

After thirty years of working there, she became paranoid. She started to keep her head down and diverted her attention from what was going on in the office. She felt panicky whenever the owner's sons came through the door. She felt like they thought they were better than her. They never did look her in the eyes. Their dad always wore Levi's and dressed casually since the company made gun parts. The atmosphere was always friendly and relaxed. May always wore Levi's as well, and a jersey with a sports logo on it.

But the sons were management now, and they were (what May called) upper class. They wore stylish up-to-date dress clothes. They never greeted anyone with a smile or said good morning as their dad had. I could tell it was starting to bother her. She didn't like them very much, with their almighty attitudes.

They called May into their office one morning and told her that they thought it was time that she retired. She was devastated. She couldn't understand why they were doing this to her. She wasn't ready to retire yet. That night, she came over to my house to tell me what had gone on that day at the office, and she was crying.

"All those things they said I was doing, aren't true. I do my work. I don't even take a lunch hour anymore! I think they're prejudiced," she said.

I knew that they had witnessed the change in May as I had. The forgetfulness and confusion. I didn't want to make her feel bad, so I just let her vent.

"What am I going to do?" she said.

"Enjoy life, May. You've earned it." I wanted to add *while you can* but decided I had better not.

As time went on, I had probably corrected May too many times. When she would stumble around searching for a word, thinking that she didn't remember it, I would fill in the blanks.

If it irritated her, she would say "I know!" and end our walk early, going into her house and slamming the door.

The next day it would all be forgotten, and we would do it all over again. Barkley had gotten so used to walking with May that he would head right over to her house right up to her front door to pick her up. He became very protective of her. If we spoke her name in our house, his ears would perk up, and he would go to the front door. We had all become very close through the years.

One time, I told May that I wished we had known each other growing up. It was funny because we both lived in the same city, and went to the same schools, but she was a few years older than me. She was the first graduating class of our new high school, and then I came along a few years later. I talked about the dances that I went to in high school, but she never interjected that she had attended any. I wondered at that time why she hadn't gone to any of the dances, since she let me know that she was a song leader for the cheer team at our school.

They were usually very popular girls. I told her I thought that was so neat that she was a song leader, but she just shrugged her shoulders like it didn't matter to her. I told her that my sister Katie, that was a year older than me, was on the dance team and would perform at the football games.

"I was so proud of her." I said, "She was so outgoing and funny." She was well-liked in school. I told her that my older sister Angel went to the same high school and could sing. She had a starring role in the play *Bye Bye Birdie*.

"She was about your age, May. Do you remember her?"

May looked down and sadly said she couldn't remember.

I told her I was the quiet sister, not outgoing at all like the other two. When I was in Acapella Choir, the teacher who had taught both my sisters assumed that I was like them, with beautiful voices, and liked to be in the limelight, but he soon found out that I was not like them at all.

I told her he had asked me to sing a solo part. "I was scared to death! So scared that it made my knees knock, which made my voice shake. I was terrible."

By then, May was laughing so hard at my story she had tears running down her face. I said, "You can bet, I was never asked to sing a solo again."

Later that night, I thought about May telling me she was a song leader in school but not wanting to talk much about it. Were the other girls mean to her? Did she feel discriminated against? I didn't want to cause her any unhappiness by asking her about it. I did, however, look at my yearbook to see if perhaps she would be in the senior section. But instead of her, her younger brother was highlighted on several of the pages for playing sports. I thought I remembered him being a senior.

I took my yearbook over to May's house, and we sat on her front porch. I showed her pictures of her brother. She surprised me by talking about some of her brother's friends. She could remember them. She asked to borrow my yearbook. She was sure there were more Japanese friends of her brother's in there. She didn't know what happened to her yearbooks. I left it with her, not knowing months later that her memory would be so bad, and she would tell me that she didn't have my yearbook when I asked for it back.

I was a person that suffered from anxiety from time to time. Mayumi provided a sense of calmness to me. Between walking and talking and the stories we would share, it was good for me. She would describe her trips to Japan and all its sights. She would tell me about the food she and her relatives would eat there. She would describe it so clearly, I could picture it perfectly in my mind. It made me feel as if I had been there. She couldn't understand why anybody that traveled so much as me and Paul, why we wouldn't have gone to Japan with all its beauty.

She definitely made me want to go there. May didn't speak Japanese, being raised in the United States, but she knew a few Japanese words and would share them with us. Whenever she tasted something good, she would say, "Oisin," meaning delicious or good tasting. May told me how she loved to go shopping in Tokyo at the Giza shopping center. She said it was a shopper's paradise. Everything was expensive, but she liked buying name-brand purses made of real leather. She would always buy several T-shirts and loved to buy fancy glassware. She told me that her family got tickets to attend a sumo wrestling match and how interesting it was to watch, but she would never go again.

The Imperial Palace was her favorite thing to see. It was still in use by the Imperial family, so they weren't allowed inside, but the East Gardens were so beautiful. She described how at a distance you could see Mt Fuji. Her cousin took them to the Kabuki-za Theater to watch performances of her Japanese heritage. I could tell though; it was the shopping and the food that she enjoyed the most. She had bought so many things that she had to pay to have them shipped home because she had already filled the empty suitcase she had taken for her shopping sprees.

The restaurant that she seemed to remember the most was one where the ladies who worked there wore kimonos, and it had a tempura counter. She told me that her sister went with her on that trip, told her she didn't like the Japanese food and didn't see why they had to have it for every meal. That did not go over well with Mayumi. It caused feelings with her cousins, and Mayumi was embarrassed by it.

"I'm never going to invite her to go to Japan ever again!"

"Would you ever want to live in Japan with your cousins?"

"I couldn't afford to, it's so expensive. I'm thankful that I can at least vacation there as often as I can.

I don't know how many more times I'll be able to go there with my memory problem."

As time went on, I heard the same story of her going to Japan and how she would never invite her sister again, and again, not remembering that she had told me this several times before. I just listened to her talk about Japan because I knew how happy it made her. If I ever reminded her that she already told me something, she would just ignore me and would go on telling me the same thing anyway, as if I wasn't there, and she was talking to someone else. Sometimes I could see this fog come over her as if she was far away. I was glad that I was with her at those times, afraid to leave her alone. I spent so much time with May now, I was getting to know everything about her. Good and bad.

It was years before May would let me in her house. When we would take food over to her, she would open her door just a tiny bit and peek out to see who was there, and then when she saw that it was me standing there with a plate of food, she would open the door wider to take the food but never inviting me in as I did with her.

Today was different. She opened her door and invited me in. I was shocked. In past times, when she would say something was not working like her fireplace, Paul would always offer to come to take a look and see what's wrong with it. She would decline the help, saying her hearth was stacked full of newspapers and that she would have her nephew look at it, but she never did.

She wanted things fixed but didn't want outsiders in her home. Today was different. She took the plate from me and led me to a small sitting room at the front of her house. The blinds were closed, all but one slat for her to peek through like she always did.

The sitting room had a floral couch, and in the corner of the room was an old scratched-up end table crowded with pots and half-dead plants. Directly in front of her window was also a three-tier glass plant stand that was missing one of its glass shelves.

The piece of furniture that she was most proud of was her china hutch. In it, she had memoirs from Japan. She brought out beautiful glass dishes; the painting on them was so intricate. She showed me her Japanese doll dressed in a kimono, and a fan that had Japanese symbols inscribed on it, but she couldn't remember what it meant anymore. I couldn't believe the Japanese vases and the rare hand-painted plates stacked on top of each other in the cabinet.

In her bedroom, she had a Tansu chest; she said it was given to her by a great uncle that would come to celebrate Chinese New Year with her mother. Her antique Kutani tea sets were my favorite. I'm sure she had no idea of their value. There was an out-of-date calendar that hung on the wall next to the china hutch. Its red and green background colors stood out against the dull white wall that needed painting. The numbers were written in Japanese. I couldn't tell what year it was from, but I'm sure it had significance to her.

When she opened the doors on the bottom of the cabinet, it hosted a pile of books with old bindings. When she reached for the books, an 8x10 hand-painted watercolor picture fell out. She brought out a couple of old books for me to see. One book was about the Japanese community and how the Japanese people in California were forced out and had to leave their homes and most of their belongings. They were taken to concentration camps in Delta, Utah. I had never heard of that before. I was shocked at the mistreatment she told me about, and she said some of the abused were ancestors of hers. I looked at her sad face and thumbed through the book looking at the black-and-white pictures of the Japanese people. She asked me if I wanted to take it home and read it since I was so interested.

CHAPTER EIGHT

....

I WAS SO FOCUSED on the history book because Mayumi had relatives that experienced this atrocity. She handed both books to me, but I told her that one was enough for now. I took it home and immediately pushed the novel I had been reading aside and began looking through the aged-worn book. I became so engrossed in the encounters and the people who were brave enough to share their stories. They told of the hard times they had and the lack of proper provisions. They explained how they had done nothing wrong, living normal everyday lives.

The only justification was they were Japanese.

I had heard all my life about the Holocaust and the heinous crimes and killings that took place against the people who were Jewish. I heard about Hitler and what a monster he was, but I never in my life had heard about the Japanese concentration camps right here in our state, one hundred and thirty miles southwest of Salt Lake City. I read that the original name was Central Utah Relocation Center. They called it Topaz.

Most of the people who lived there came from San Francisco, California.

There were twelve barracks, a mess hall, a latrine, a place to do laundry, and a recreation hall. Mayumi was told that there was no privacy for her relatives and that the barracks had no running water either.

There was only one light, and the small area was heated by a coal stove. One room would house an entire family. Cots were placed along the walls, but there wasn't any other furniture. Not a nightstand, not a privacy screen. If they had to go to the bathroom, they had to go outside to the latrine.

May fought hard to bring back the stories that her relatives talked about when they were together. Her great Auntie Suki was a nurse living with her husband and two kids in California. Her husband was a manager of an upscale restaurant in San Francisco. They had two beautiful Japanese daughters that were attending a private school and were already planning to go to college. They were a respected family in their community with a nice house and a large vegetable garden in the backyard that they used in their father's restaurant.

The furnishings in the house were expensive. Brocade couches that faced each other with a black lacquer table between them. On the walls were antique Asian hand-carved wood wall panels.

May said, "I was told that they did well for themselves."

She said the order was issued for all people of Japanese descent to leave their homes, their places of employment, and the schools that their children were attending. Everything they had worked so hard for.

They couldn't believe it; they were given only six hours to leave. They all cried and tried to think of where they could hide, but it was no use. It was an order from the government.

How could this happen? They were Japanese American, most born and raised in the United States.

In 1842, then US President Franklin D. Roosevelt signed an executive order, and there was nothing they could do about it. They had no choice but to pack what they could carry and leave. The most challenging aspect of living in the barracks was the complete lack of privacy. The residents were administered exams to prove their loyalty. They wanted the Japanese people to swear their allegiance to the United States. The exams were made to help the war department, but instead, inflicted deep resentment among those who were born in Japan and had been denied American citizenship.

She cried when she told me her ancestors were fenced in for three long years. They were traumatized by the whole thing. Even after they were released and returned to their private lives, nothing was the same for them. They still faced discrimination from the Americans and had financial problems.

"My auntie was able to get back to work as a nurse," she said, "but my uncle had health problems from living in the camp and the manual labor they required of him."

The family was never the same after that. Her grandmother cried when she told her of the hardships she had endured.

I felt like I needed to say something in response to that sad but true story, so I told her about how at my sister Katie's funeral, our old neighbors came to pay their respects. My parents had already passed on.

Our neighbor said, "We really liked your dad. He was a good man."

"Thank you, I loved him a lot."

He continued, "I remember when the house was for sale, and your folks came to look at it. I said to my wife, 'oh my hell, a Black person's looking at that house.' Of course, after they bought the house, I realized he wasn't black at all, he was Mexican."

He went on to say nice things about my dad as if that would make me feel any better. I never got over him saying that. They did like our family; I knew that because I used to babysit his kids, but I felt totally different about him after that.

"Discrimination is everywhere," I said to May. "Not only racial discrimination but also against fat people, possibly assuming that they are lazy. Then, discrimination of religion if you don't believe the same as they do.

"Discrimination of gender is a big one right now. Gay people are tired of hiding who they truly are; they just want to be accepted and be able to love who they choose to love and be with whom they chose."

We sat in silence for a few minutes, but then I said, "Oh, even discrimination against disabled people."

"The real estate agent that helped us find our house is a friend of mine. She owned a one-level house with a big backyard that was perfect for people with disabilities. The state contracts with a company to offer provider services, a provider is a person who can help with such things as taking the disabled person grocery shopping, helping with dinner, personal hygiene, and in some cases having the overnight staff there to make sure they were safe while they slept."

Gracie, my friend said, "They were good renters for her, but the neighbors started to complain."

They didn't want "those kinds of people" living next to them. The provider company tried to talk to the neighbor, but they didn't want to hear it.

They would call my friend, the owner of the rental home, and complain about knit picky things and even call the police on them. One neighbor even pulled a gun on one of the autistic young men that wandered into his yard to see his chickens.

It caused the provider so much stress they decided after a year, it just wasn't worth it anymore. The neighbors had made it clear they didn't want them there.

My friend ended up selling the house.

Both May and my family had experienced what discrimination felt like, and we bonded because of that.

My ancestors immigrated to the United States from Chihuahua, Mexico. A civil war was going on in Mexico at that time, and there were a lot of different groups fighting against each other for control.

Everyone had to choose a side.

My great-grandfather chose to support the government and fought when he was needed. They didn't like the battles and didn't feel safe so decided to flee from their village along with others.

They made it to the United States border. My great-grandmother had all of their papers in order, but it was hard for a young mom in a strange country with two little girls.

She found a place to live in a rooming house and a job as a cook in Idaho for a company that hired migrant workers.

My great-grandfather came later and went to work in a mine, but he didn't like it very much. After living there for three years, they moved to Utah, where they not only worked full-time jobs but attended night school to learn English, and eventually were able to get their citizenship papers.

I finished reciting our family history, and it was time for me to leave. She walked me out, and we started down her front steps.

"May, where are your glasses?"

"I can't find them," she said.

Suddenly, she fell down her front porch steps right in front of me. I tried to catch her, but I just wasn't fast enough.

I tried to help her up, but she cried out that her leg hurt. I carefully lifted her arm, so she could grab hold of me.

When she finally got up, she complained, "I can't walk on it."

I helped her into the house, grateful she was so small.

She hobbled over to the couch and dropped down, moaning the entire time. She tried to push the footstool over, but she was in too much pain to lift her leg.

I knew I better go get Paul. He dropped everything and came right over.

"Her leg might be broken." I told him she didn't have her glasses on and might have been disoriented.

"Her eyesight isn't that good even with her glasses," said Paul.

We asked her if she would be able to put shorter pants on, so we could take a look at her leg.

"Maybe, if Marcelina can help me."

Paul went out onto the front porch to give us some privacy. "Let me know when I can come back in."

May told me where to look for a pair of capris.

In her bedroom, I found piles of clothes on the floor. I grabbed the closest pair.

She managed to shimmy out of her long pants hanging on to me in her dingy stretched-out underwear that hung on her skinny bones.

Her family was always telling her that she needed to eat, and she would tell them that she did, but it was evident, she obviously was not eating enough.

I then told her to steady herself against me and slightly lifted her leg into the short pant leg. She didn't cry out, but I could tell she was in pain.

Once she was changed, Paul came back into the house. No bones were sticking out, thank goodness.

Paul applied pressure up and down her leg and on the lower half of her leg, she yelled out in pain.

"I think we better take her to Insta Care."

Paul picked May up, carried her to my car, and helped her inside. Even though May was a small person, it still took strength for him to carry her out to the car. It was times like this that I was glad he continued working out at the gym.

On the way to Insta Care, I asked May if she wanted to call her brother and let him know what had happened.

She said she couldn't find her phone.

"You can use mine." I handed it to her.

I glanced at her in the back seat. She was holding my phone, but she just stared at it and didn't ask for any help.

I didn't say anything to her, I just kept driving.

I would wait until we got inside the waiting room and call him myself. May tried to stand when the receptionist called her name but couldn't.

"She needs a wheelchair," I said a little too forcibly.

They brought her one, and I pushed her over to the cubicle, so they could get her insurance information. The lady asked Mayumi her full name, and Mayumi told her.

She asked for her date of birth, but May couldn't remember it. The nice lady then asked Mayumi if she had an insurance card. She looked unsure but started searching in her wallet.

She brought out several cards like she was fanning out a deck of cards.

The lady reached over and picked one out. It had expired.

Then the receptionist asked if it was okay for her to look through them. May looked relieved.

Sadly, May looked confused with most of the questions they asked.

Was it my responsibility to tell them that she had Alzheimer's, or in her profession could she tell?

I knew one thing; I was not leaving her side.

When they called her back, Mayumi looked scared.

When the nurse started to wheel her back, I followed.

She asked me, "Are you family?" She knew damn well I wasn't family by the looks of us.

"I am." I know she didn't believe me, but she didn't say another word.

Paul waited in the waiting room. The doctor came in and asked her what happened, and instead of answering, she looked over at me.

"She didn't have her glasses on and fell down her front porch stairs. She may have been dizzy."

The doctor asked her why she didn't have her glasses on, and he looked right at her, not me.

"I can't find them," she said.

He was checking her leg as we spoke and asked her, "When was the last time you had an eye exam?"

She didn't say anything, and I butted in. "She doesn't see that well anyway."

He said, "Maybe it's time for new glasses."

She didn't respond, but she cried out when he checked her lower leg.

He rolled his chair back. "Let's get some X-rays done on this."

He called for his nurse to take May to the X-ray room. I stood, and he said, "They'll only be a few minutes."

So, I sat back down.

After the nurse rolled her out, I said to the doctor, "She has Alzheimer's and gets scared."

He answered in a singsong way, "I know she does, she'll be fine with Nancy."

I waited patiently and thought about calling May's brother, but I didn't know if I had enough time before they got back and decided against it.

Nancy rolled May back into the room, and the doctor came back and looked at the X-rays. It was good news; she just had a bad sprain.

I think I was happier about that than May was.

When we went back to the waiting room where Paul was, he said, "I called May's brother, he's going to meet us at her house."

We helped May out to our car, and Paul lifted her back inside.

I asked her if she wanted me to go through a fast-food drive to get her something to eat.

She was excited. "Oh yeah, that would be good."

"What are you in the mood for?"

As usual, she couldn't decide; so, I suggested cheeseburgers, fries, and milkshakes, and we drove home to eat them.

When we got to May's house, her brother was waiting on the same stairs she had fallen. He came over to help Paul get her out of the car.

May was more worried about getting her fast food than telling her brother what had happened.

I gave him the details, and I told him that the doctor recommended May get an eye exam.

He thanked us for helping her. By then, May had her leg up on a footrest and was eating her fast food. I handed May's brother the paperwork from Insta Care and the doctor's recommendations, and Paul and I went home.

Paul asked, "When we were at the Insta Care, did you notice that May wasn't even able to answer when her birth date was?"

"I did. I'm so concerned about her, honey. I can see her declining more and more. She's getting more dependent on me now and can't help but allow it."

Paul said, "Just be glad that you're retired and have the time to help her."

"I know. I am." The next thing I know, he leaned over and kissed me on the forehead.

"It's really nice of you to do the things you do to help her, Mar."

It choked me up to hear him say that to me.

May's physical body was in good health. She was not overweight; she didn't have diabetes. She walked seven days a week, sometimes twice a day out of boredom, even in the heat of the summer, or in the cold of winter.

It was important to her to stay active, but what was not in good health was her brain. May was well aware at one time that she had a brain tumor that was inoperable and then diagnosed with Alzheimer's.

She didn't seem to be concerned about having either one. She went about her life as routinely as she could. Her doctor had started her on medication for her Alzheimer's, but she didn't always remember to take it. Her family hired a college student that would come over once a week and set her pills up, but she would forget what day it was and forget to take them.

She had told me she didn't want anyone to know that she had forgotten them, so before she came again, she would throw them in the garbage. What she really needed was for someone to give her the medications and watched that she took them.

Family members that came to see her would generally bring her fast food. She loved it. Hamburgers, hotdogs, fries, milkshakes, pizza, it all made her happy since she didn't cook. She told me one time on our walk that she ate healthily.

I teasingly said, "I like the diet that you're on."

She didn't think that was very funny. She ate what she wanted, and at this stage of the game, who knew what the future held for her anyway.

We certainly didn't help her much either. I liked to bake, and Paul loved his desserts, so I was always taking cookies, slices of pie, or pieces of cake over to her. The smile on her face when I would hand it to her made me glad that we had shared it with our good friend.

May always wanted what everybody else had. If they got a new roof, she thought she needed one and would tell her brother. We had a neighbor that got a new patio put in. She also wanted that, even though she didn't use the small patio she had.

Anytime Paul and I went to the nursery to get plants, we would usually take May with us because she enjoyed it so much. She wanted to buy everything there, but her vegetables for her garden had to be certain ones, Japanese eggplants, Japanese cucumbers, and special cherry tomatoes.

May was crouched down in her front yard pulling weeds when we pulled into our driveway.

I said, "Oh no, the one time we don't invite her to go with us, and she's going to see all these plants." Of course, she wandered over watching us and asking where we had been. I felt bad that we didn't ask her to go with us.

As we carried the plants back through the gate into the backyard, she tagged along right behind us.

Once we were in the backyard, May said, "I wish my backyard looked like this."

Against the white vinyl fence was a nicely trimmed area sectioned off by cement curbing. There were lush green plants, maroon-colored bayberry, and bright green ferns that had made it through the cold winter to surprise us with their new spring growth.

It was a beautiful day to plant our flowers. May wanted to be a part of it all. She followed Paul around from spot to spot trying to help him but couldn't keep the colors straight, so Paul would tell her which plant came next. The red petunia came first, then the purple one, then a pink one, and last the yellow marigold.

She finally understood the order that Paul was planting them, and she had them out of the carton ready to go.

I told May, "If we have any flowers left over when we're done, we can plant the rest of them in your backyard."

She was excited. "Okay," and followed Paul around like a dutiful child.

I was finishing trimming up our roses when I noticed that they were at the end of the curbing, and they only had three flowers left. What good would that do her? I felt bad that I made her the offer.

Despite her memory problem, she hadn't forgotten about planting the leftover flowers in her backyard. Paul was sweaty and tired, but he knew how much it meant to her. He grabbed his shovel and his hoe, and I picked up the few remaining flowers, and we walked over to May's backyard.

She had a white vinyl fence like everyone did in our neighborhood. Paul had fixed her vinyl gate when it was broken years ago. Paul asked her where she wanted them planted, and she took the longest time deciding as if it was a major decision, instead of three measly petunias.

Finally, I piped up, feeling tired of standing there in the sun. I pointed to a spot directly across from her sliding glass door that led to her kitchen. "How about here? Then you can look out your window and will be able to see the color."

She thought that was a great idea. We almost hated

for May to see us plant anything in our yard because we knew that she would hit her brother up to take her to the nursery to buy the same thing we had.

He was a busy man because he owned his own electronics company. Even though he might not take her immediately, he would always follow through with taking her and would always buy her lunch while they were out too.

The next day when May was over, and Paul was at the gym, I had my stereo playing the Beatles in the background. In between our conversations, she would listen to the music and shake her shoulders back and forth and would sing some of the lyrics, or when she couldn't remember the words, she would hum to the music.

I asked May if she liked the Beatles in her teenage years, and she said, "Oh yes!"

Then she asked me, "What are you playing that music on?"

I took her into our extra bedroom at the back of our house to show her the music room that I had made. It had a stereo that played an iPod as well as the radio.

I had stacks of organized CDs of various genres, music DVDs, and a Bose speaker that I used when I opened up the bedroom window to blast the music outside when we were having a party.

85

She said, "I'd like to listen to music once in a while."

I asked her, "Do you have a radio?"

She said, "Yes."

Her radio had been programmed to a sports channel since she was such a sports enthusiast. I told her about when I was a teenager I was so into music.

I had a portable record player that my parents had given me for Christmas.

"It meant so much to me, that I cried when I opened it.

"I would take it outside in the summer and play the 45 records I bought with my babysitting money. I would sit on our lawn with that thing cranked up as high as I could get it."

I said, "And would sing along with the music."

Then May asked me, "Can you help me change the station on my radio to an oldies station like yours?"

I said, "Sure." We walked across the lawn to her house and went inside.

Amongst the mess in the hall sat her old dusty radio on the floor, with a sportscaster talking about an upcoming game and the players. Mismatched slippers and shoes lay about the room.

A fairly nice chair was shoved into the hall with stacks of jackets piled high, and miscellaneous items on the side of them, not allowing entrance to the bedroom where her mother once slept. From what she had explained about it some time ago, the room seemed like a shrine to her mother.

She was the only one that went in there.

I remember telling her that she should make use of that room since it was just a two-bedroom house. I said, "You can pick a new bedspread out on Amazon, and I'll order it for you.

"You could organize your crafts on some new shelves, and I can help you decorate them."

She hesitantly answered, "Maybe."

But I knew it would never come to fruition. May's parents had been dead for years, and nothing ever changed in that house. Having a chair blocking that room had a weird feeling about it. I set her radio to the oldies station that was playing The Beach Boys, "Help Me Rhonda."

She excitedly said, "Right there, that will be good." I left her there listening to music and went home. Later that night as I lay in my bed, I could picture the inside of her house and thought of ways I wanted to help her redecorate things and make her surroundings safer.

I worried about her tripping on the clutter. How was I going to word it, so as not to offend her?

After all, her older brother had said to us, "Believe

me, she's a true-blue hoarder."

I did get her to go to a container store that carried every kind of storage container you'd ever want or need. May did buy several see-through containers that had rolling wheels with clear drawers so that you could see what was inside.

I encouraged her to get that one for sure, saying she could put her yarn in there. I thought, YES, this is a start! Days later I said, "Do you want me to come over and help you organize things in your new containers?"

She replied, "No, I can do it."

I asked her, "Where did you put them?"

"Downstairs."

I thought, well, that's the last of those, she'll forget she even has them.

CHAPTER NINE

....

OUR COMMUNITY had an event every year called Harvest Days. People would meet at the Bowery for a celebration, where they served hamburgers, hotdogs, and had games and drawings and a local talent show. We invited May to go with us. It looked like they had a pretty good turnout, as we tried to find a parking space. We drove around a couple of times until we saw someone leave and hurried into their parking spot.

The three of us walked over to get in line to get our food, while our eyes searched for familiar faces from our immediate neighborhood. May spotted a couple that was sitting together at a long banquet table covered with butcher paper. She pointed them out to me. They smiled and waved at us, and May left the line to walk over to say hello.

They were the Nicholsons and had lived in the neighborhood as long as May had. They were the original owners of their house, as she was.

The Nicholsons embraced May, and they talked for a while. They were well aware of May's diagnosis as were most of the neighbors by now.

They always hugged her when we walked around the block. I worried as the line moved forward, to the point that Paul and I were choosing our food. I didn't want May to have to go back to the end of the line, so I picked up an extra paper plate and began pushing it along the table that had all the condiments on it.

I selected a hamburger bun, not knowing if she wanted a hamburger or a hotdog. I put catsup and mustard on it, making it the same as mine. I looked over my shoulder and could see that she was still visiting with our neighbors.

I selected a bag of chips for her and headed to sit down with my plate stacked on top of hers, and the bag of chips between my teeth. So many people were saving places for family members that it was hard to find seats for the three of us to sit.

I saw May look over at the line, searching for us. She looked nervous at not being able to see us. I called out to her across the tables and showed her that I had two full plates. She hurried over. I said, "Why don't you go get us a drink from that tub of sodas over there," and she did.

We finally wedged in between two families and ate our meals. She talked about the neighbors that she visited with, and how nice they always were to her. Saying for about the fifth time that they were the original owners of their home like she was, and how they were the first ones to build in our neighborhood, which she had already told me.

When we finished eating our meal, they announced that Bingo would be starting. They started handing out Bingo cards while Paul was throwing away our trash. Some people took two cards to have a better chance of winning. I looked at the prize table that was loaded with really nice items.

Definitely, an incentive to play to win. Paul was back, and I had already placed a card on the table for him, whether he wanted to play or not. May was excited that we were staying to play. She was so happy to be out. They were now handing out the beans we were going to use as place markers.

The spokesperson was a round man with a balding head and had the perfect voice to announce the game was going to begin. I looked around the room, and everyone's faces were looking down studying their Bingo cards, but May.

She was studying the people to see if she knew anyone else there, probably wondering why there weren't any Japanese people in attendance. They called the first number B55, and I looked over at May's card. She had that number but hadn't noticed.

I reached over and grabbed one of her beans and placed it on the number and another one on the free spot. She looked down but didn't say anything to me. As the game went on and numbers were called, I noticed that her card was almost empty. I couldn't play my card and keep track of hers at the same time. Soon someone yelled Bingo!

May looked disappointed. She couldn't concentrate very well, so I asked her if she wanted to go watch some of the presentations in the far corner of the park where they had policemen with their K9s, but she wanted to play another game of Bingo.

Some people kept their same cards and others exchanged theirs for new ones and so did May. This time when a number was called, I looked at her card first, and then mine, then I would show her where to place the bean.

She started paying attention to her card, even though she couldn't see very well. I soon fell behind on my card and was just helping her play. She only needed one more number to win. Somebody called Bingo, and we both said, "Oh No!" almost too loudly.

They had the person read back the numbers that were called, and she had missed a number and gotten it wrong, so they continued with the game.

Finally, May's card was full, and I said in a hurry, "Yell Bingo!"

She was embarrassed, but she did.

I helped her recite back the numbers, and she had won. They congratulated her and told her that she could go up to the front of the stage where the prize table was and choose something.

She walked up to the table and stared at all the options, not sure which one to take. I didn't dare embarrass her by going up to help her choose. They were very patient with her. I was so surprised that out of all the things she could have chosen, she picked a cooler.

I leaned over and said to Paul, "Why would she choose a cooler?"

Maybe it was because it was the largest prize available. I wasn't sure, but she was so pleased that she had won, it didn't matter.

On an evening in August, the news had forecast that we were going to get a pretty intense storm. They said that we were going to get winds up to seventy miles an hour with thunderstorms.

We tried to prepare for the storm by making sure everything that could blow away was put in the shed. I didn't see May that day, and as the evening went on, the dark clouds started to roll in.

We watched out our front windows at the lightning, and then the thunder began to crack. It was a loud thunder that rumbled the house and made our dog nervous. The first thing I thought of was May. I knew that she would be nervous and scared too, but I hoped that her TV would keep her distracted.

It was getting late now, as the lightning flashed in the half-moon window above our glass sliding door. It was about time for the nine o'clock news when the power went out. We peered through the blinds out into the neighborhood, to make sure that everybody's power was out, not just ours. Just as we expected, everybody's house was black.

Paul shuffled around looking for a flashlight but couldn't see in the dark to find one. We decided even if it was earlier than we normally went to bed, we would go anyway. I peeked out of the bathroom window that faced May's house and saw that it, too, was pitch black.

I thought about calling her cell phone but decided that maybe she would be asleep already. I knew that she would be frightened if she was still awake. Instead, I went to bed and lay there listening to the hard rain hit the windows, rattling, and sounding as if it would break them.

The wind continued blowing hard, and I could see from my open blinds as I lay there, that the trees were bending over as if they were going to snap. We didn't have any large trees in our yard, but the neighbor had plenty. We had just fallen asleep when our doorbell rang. We both jumped up in a panic, expecting to see May at our door with a frantic expression on her face. But it was Jake our other neighbor, explaining that the Andersen's to the west of us had two trees blow over on their fence.

He wanted to know if Paul had a chainsaw. When Paul went back into the bedroom to get dressed, Jake told me, "I knew that if anyone in the neighborhood had a chainsaw, it would be Paul."

He probably thought that because Paul was older than most of our neighbors, yet they would see him doing his trimming. They'd see him up on top of a tall ladder trimming the fitzers, and I would be down below holding the ladder as if it would do any good to keep him from falling.

When Paul was ready, he and Jake went through the back gate to our shed. That's where he kept all his yard tools and his mower and the chainsaw. He picked it up, and they headed into the pelting rain to the Andersen's house. People were standing around shivering in the cold night air. Some had hoodies pulled up over their heads, while others had ball caps on to protect their faces from the rain.

I heard the chainsaw start up, as I cranked my

neck to see out to the neighbor's yard. It must have been far enough west that I couldn't see what was going on, but I could hear the whining of the saw. I pictured the bits of wood that would fly through the air as the saw gnawed through the timber. I had helped Paul enough times when he used that chainsaw, that I could remember the splinters that would fall on my shoulders and my head while he was up on the ladder, trying to not look up to protect my eyes.

The neighbors were all so good to pull together on such a stormy night. I was glad when Paul was able to come home safely. He was soaked and tired. I said to him, "Go take a hot shower, and we'll go back to bed."

By the next morning, the storm had moved on, and the sun was out. Like always, May was out in her front yard.

She was looking down at her flowers. "The rain has almost destroyed my plants."

"I know, hopefully, they'll come out of it. We had damage to ours as well."

She said that the lightning and thunder had scared her, and she went to bed and pulled the blankets over her head. Her hair looked like it too.

Her hair was starting to look pretty wild.

I asked her, "Would you like me to cut and color your hair for you?

"I did hair many years ago when my kids were little. Do you remember me telling you that? I had a basement beauty salon that Paul built for me. I was able to stay home with our kids and still bring in a little bit of income. I enjoyed doing hair back then and was able to grow my little business into a full-time job. I was proud that I had a good clientele, and it worked well to be able to work at home."

I think because I told May that I had a good business, she felt okay about letting me do her hair. She did mention, though, that her hairdresser who normally did her hair was a Japanese girl.

I felt the pressure of having to prove that I was just as good as her.

I no longer had a beauty salon in my house, which had been eons ago, but I never lost the love of doing hair. I still knew what I was doing.

I cut her hair into a cute china doll cut and colored it a shiny black. I washed, dried it, and turned the ends under to a soft curl. She really did look darling, and she smiled as she looked in the mirror.

I asked her if she wanted me to put a little bit of makeup on her since she told me that she was going to a family party that night. She consented to let me do it, as long as it was light and not too much, she said.

I was very careful about what I did to her, making sure it was a soft look, but adding a little color to her face. Even the face cream I put on her sun-drenched skin seemed to soften the lines on her face, and the black mascara seemed to brighten her eyes.

She didn't normally wear makeup and was surprised when she looked in the mirror and saw how nice she looked. I think she felt pretty because when she went home, she changed into some floral capris and a capped-sleeve blouse and had to come back to show me.

I was so happy that I was able to make her feel good about herself.

The next day while May and I walked, she told me that her family told her how nice she looked, and they were surprised that I was the one who did it for her. They couldn't believe that she hadn't gone to the Japanese hairdresser where they all went.

She was so proud to tell them that it had only cost her a box of hair coloring. They laughed and said, "Maybe we should start having her do *our* hair."

Any day that she could go someplace, she would say, "That was a good day."

We wore face masks everywhere we went because of the pandemic. Whenever May would get in my car, the first thing I would say to her was, "Do you have a mask in your purse? We have to wear our masks."

She didn't remember to get one. She would have to get back out of the car and unlock her front door with the key that she had tied to a piece of yarn that she wore around her neck. It would take forever for her to come out, so I would have to shut the car off, get out, walk across the lawn, where the front door would be left wide open, and she would be standing there, rummaging through her worn-out purse to see if there was a mask in there. She would usually drop it on the floor and go to the next purse that she had dug out.

Finally, after going through three purses, I said, "I think I have an extra one in my glove compartment." My concern was that since we had to wear masks *everywhere*, if I kept sharing with May, *we* wouldn't have any.

It wasn't that she didn't have enough masks. Her sister was a seamstress and made masks for her and made one for me as well. She made masks of different patterns and colors, and May had plenty of them, but she never remembered to put them back in her purse when she took them off. May told me that the masks her sister made for her were different than mine.

She said they were made to fit an Asian face. I asked her what she meant by that, and she showed me how she didn't have any bone in her nose, and when she put a regular mask on and put the elastic around each ear, it would pull the mask tight, flattening her nose. We both laughed. I wouldn't have known that.

CHAPTER TEN

······················

ONE DAY when May and I were out walking on a fairly busy street, we saw Mr. Overalls. Paul named him that because he always wore jean overalls and a long-sleeved shirt. It was his distinguishing characteristic because he dressed like that year around.

He shuffled through our neighborhood every day wearing his muddy work boots and carrying his walking stick.

He was in his front yard watering his newly planted flowers. We said good morning, and he called us over.

He shut off his water, wiped his damp wrinkled hands on his overalls, and smiled a toothless smile. He asked us to follow him into his backyard.

He proudly showed us his incredible garden. Rows and rows of cultivated vegetables; onions, beets, lettuce, and radishes. He pointed out that potatoes were planted under the ground. Pear and peach trees lined the garden perimeter.

Mr. Overalls told us when his wife was alive, they bottled or canned everything they could and lived off it all winter long. Even though she had been gone for a few years, he still canned much of the produce and fruit.

Of course, May was astounded by his garden. She kept asking him questions, but he ignored her and went on showing us more.

However, when I asked a question, he would look right at me and answer. Maybe it was because Mr. Overalls was hard of hearing, and May had a soft voice.

He was ninety years old, and as far as I know, he had been a hard worker his entire life. He told us he had always been a gardener.

When I asked him who helped him plant, he pointed to his puffed-out chest and boastfully said, "Me!"

He went on to tell us he was out in his yard at six o'clock every morning. He said his son tilled the dirt for him, but he did all the planting himself.

His rows were straight and uniform, and the plants were watered by tall, strategically placed sprinklers.

He showed us a porch he had built that he closed in with see-through plastic. He left an open window, so he could see his garden.

Inside was an old beat-up easy chair where he informed us, he took afternoon naps. Next to the chair were boxes of white onions, garlic, and potatoes from last year's crop.

Mr. Overalls reached into the box and pulled out two onions, one for each of us. May was thrilled. I thought that was funny since she didn't cook.

I thanked him and told him we needed to be on our way, and that I didn't want my dog to go potty on his vegetables.

"Come around back any time you're out walking." And Mr. Overalls went back to his beautiful garden.

May looked pleased with hearing that, so when we were out front far enough away that I was sure he couldn't hear me, I said, "Please, May, even though he is lonely and invited us, don't try to walk to his house by yourself. I don't want you to get lost."

We continued our walk and talked about how we couldn't believe he was ninety years old and still living on his own.

Mr. Overalls was a tall, broad man with weathered skin from the sun, and had told us that he worked construction in his younger years. It was amazing to us that he could still get down on his knees and plant a garden.

When we got back from our walk, I told Paul about our visit with Mr. Overalls. He knew right away who I was talking about. I knew May was mesmerized by him as well as had respect for him and his hard work ethic.

"He is an amazing man," said May. "He gave me this onion. I hope I can be like him when I get older."

Paul and I looked at each other with uncertainty.

As time went on, May and I became extremely close. We confided in one another. I didn't know if I confided in her because I didn't think she would remember the personal things that I told her because of her having memory problems, or if I needed a confidant to express all my built-up feelings to.

I told her one day on our walk to the park that I had a younger brother that committed suicide. She didn't even know that I had a younger brother. "I never talk about him."

She looked surprised. I told her how close I was with him when we were young. "He was so handsome with his wavy black hair and small brown eyes. He had one deep dimple at the bottom of his chin when he smiled, which the girls found very attractive. He also played the guitar."

I told her about the letter addressed to me that he had left behind, and it had blood splatters on it. His letter said, "he just couldn't do it anymore."

He had some health problems and dealt with depression. He had been divorced for many years. He had a heart attack the year prior and was told to stop smoking, which he tried, but couldn't kick the habit. He couldn't continue working the strenuous job that he had, so he quit, thinking that he could qualify for physical disability assistance but was never able to receive help.

I looked over at May. She was crying. By that time, so was I.

I had never told anyone about my brother's suicide. It was too hard for me to even think about. It was easier to pretend that I didn't have a brother. She told me that she was so sorry, and she hugged me, which made us both cry even harder.

I sobbed, "I never saw it coming. He was trying so hard, working two lower-paying jobs to be able to pay his rent. He was on a very expensive heart medication that he couldn't afford. A few times he borrowed money from me and always paid me back on his payday. That was very important to him. I wished he had talked to someone, or me, about the pain and suffering he was going through. I would have told him that his life was worth living.

"I didn't know that his car had been repossessed. I'm sure that was the thing that pushed him over the edge."

I told her it felt good to talk about him, I loved him so much. I told her I felt guilty that I hadn't done more to help him, but I really tried. "I think his depression was stronger than I was."

We talked about depression, and how so many people go untreated and walk down that long dark path alone, never even realizing that it's depression. May told me that she wondered if she had depression.

She said, "I've never gotten over my mother dying at home all alone."

She had left her mom by herself and gone on a trip to San Antonio with some girlfriends. She felt as guilty as I did.

May was so lucid that day that she really was a comfort to me. It was as if she didn't even have Alzheimer's. I was truly thankful for her friendship and thankful that we could share things so close to our hearts.

As the tears continued to run down my cheeks, I talked more about my brother and his love of music. "He was in a band when he was young," I said. "They would practice in my parent's garage. I loved to listen to them play. They were really good. One day, they asked me if I wanted to join their band and play the tambourine. I couldn't believe he was including me. I was elated!

"That first practice, I tried to get the feel of the

tambourine and how to shake it, as I sang along. We sounded good harmonizing together. They were asked to play at a neighborhood dance. I was nervous for all of us, but things went well. It was a relief when kids came out on the dance floor, connecting with the music.

"It wasn't a long gig, but we were performing, and that was encouraging," I told May.

She asked, "How long did you guys stay together?"

"I can't remember exactly, but about a year, and then he had a disagreement with one of the band members, and they broke up. So that was it, but he and I always stayed close. Because I became a cosmetologist, I usually saw him every few weeks for his haircuts, and it was nice to visit with him while I cut his hair. We would see each other at our mom and dad's for Sunday dinners since he lived with them for years after his divorce. He was with them when each one of them died at home, years apart from one another. That was extremely hard on him back then."

We sat in silence for several minutes.

I suddenly thought about May being alone, so I asked her, "Do you feel sad a lot?"

She timidly replied, "Sometimes."

I could see why her isolation might cause depression, as well as not being able to do things for herself anymore.

I tried to make her feel better. "We all experience times when we feel down, May. I have been on an antidepressant for years, and it helps me."

I wanted to store that in my mind, so I would remember to bring it up with her brother the next time I saw him. I checked on her every day after that, not wanting what happened to my brother to happen to her.

CHAPTER ELEVEN

....

OCTOBER CAME, and I took May to a place called Gardner Village with rows of little stores.

Each store was decorated for Halloween in orange and black, with Paper Mache witches all around the grounds.

It was so festive. They had hot soups and sandwiches made with freshly baked bread for lunch at the Village Bakery.

The smell of the bread consumed us as we stepped inside the bakery. Rows and rows of homemade desserts were lined up ready to put in the glass case to be viewed by the mouthwatering shoppers. I went first to order. I knew May would order whatever I did because she wouldn't be able to read the overhead menu or decide, for that matter.

I tried to read it out loud to her but knew that she would still order the same as me.

She offered to pay for mine since she was having

so much fun, but I said, "No, I'm going to get it. You can get our desserts when we're ready okay?"

I didn't want anyone to ever think that was the reason I took her places, to have her pay my way. I found us a table while May went over to the self-serve to get her tea.

It really was fun to sit there and enjoy our lunch while we watched mothers shuffling in with their kids dressed in Halloween costumes.

After we finished, May remembered that she was going to get us a treat and asked, "What do you want for your dessert? I'll go get them."

"I'll have the sugar cookie frosted to look like a pumpkin." She got off her stool and walked over to the glass case while I watched her.

She ordered my sugar cookie and then appeared overwhelmed by all the choices. I looked out the window at the small stage outside. Kids in orange and black striped tights danced to the "Monster Mash." I watched how uninhibited they were, dancing around. Their parents looked so proud of them.

I enjoyed watching for a short time and glanced back up at May, wondering what was taking her so long. She was at the cash register now and was frantically digging in her purse. I could see by the stressed look on her face that something was wrong; she couldn't find her credit card.

By now, the line went out the door, and more people were lining up behind her. I knew that would make her feel more pressured.

I didn't want to leave our table to help her because I knew with how crowded it was someone would take our table right away and leave us nowhere to sit.

I waited and watched. In a trembling voice, she said to the cashier, "I can't find my credit card." She pulled out three smaller wallets from her purse, searching their slots. Then she dug deeper into her purse.

I noticed that her hands were shaking, and she was near tears. I had to go to her rescue.

"Here let me pay for it for right now. When things settle down, you can take everything out of your purse and look for it."

She said, "Okay," still very concerned about her charge card.

I asked the salesgirl, "How much does she owe you?"

"Thirty-six dollars and forty-three cents."

I looked at her in shock, "for two desserts?"

She held up two plastic bags full of sweets. May had bought one of almost everything.

I handed the girl the money, while May was still digging through her purse. She was so upset that she didn't even want to sit and enjoy one of the many desserts she had bought.

We went outside, and her whole mood changed. I could tell that she wanted to just go home.

I had spent my last forty dollars on her sweets and didn't have any more cash, so I wouldn't be doing any more shopping.

I asked her, "Do you want to go home?"

"Yes."

The whole way home she was quiet. I knew she was trying hard to remember when she had last used her charge card. I asked her if she had gotten her card back from the shop where she had purchased the porcelain witch.

She thought about it, and said, "I think I did."

I reminded her that she bought Halloween decorations at Walmart the day before.

I said, "Did you get your card back from them?"

She looked blank. I knew that she wasn't going to be able to backtrack her purchases. It was all too overwhelming for her. Who knew how long it had been missing, and she hadn't noticed? Or which charge card she had even used, she had more than one.

When we got home, she jumped right out of the car with her packages and headed across the lawn to her house. She didn't say thanks, or anything else, and closed the door.

The next day, I asked her if she found her card, and she said, "No. I called my nephew and asked him to cancel my Visa card because I lost it."

I thought she should have given it more time so that she could search more because it could be anywhere in her cluttered house.

I didn't see her until the day before Halloween. I was out on my front porch, rearranging my decorations that had been up since the first of October when May walked over to see what I was doing. I told her that I was trying to make sure nothing was in the way of the trick-or-treaters that would be coming the next evening. She hadn't put out any of the decorations that she had bought, and I never saw the expensive ceramic witch again. Probably stuck downstairs in the overflow of things she didn't know what to do with.

I asked her if she needed me to take her to get candy for the trick-or-treaters. "No, I'm just going to keep my lights off."

I was surprised because she always enjoyed seeing the little kids come to her door dressed up in their costumes.

I asked about the credit card again, and she said that her family had ordered her a new one, and it would be coming in the mail.

I knew if she needed anything, she could use the cash she had hidden in her house if she could remember where it was hidden.

In the meantime, I tried to keep her away from stores. That was the second time she had lost a credit card. Her family had to put a stop on the old card again, and the bank had to issue a new one.

At the end of our street, there is a house that's on the state's registry for historic homes. The man who owns it was so willing to let Paul and me take a tour even though it was not meant for tours.

Inside they tried hard to keep it as close to the same as they could during restoration.

A stained-glass window with red, green, and blue glass glimmered when the sunlight shined through. You had to duck your head at the top of the rock stairs leading to the first bedroom.

It had an antique bed and a nightstand of some sort that had a wash basin on it. The room next to it was wallpapered in a flowery beige-colored fabric. An old roll desk had been slid into the corner of the room which allowed more space for a bed.

The red, white, and blue patriotic colored patchwork quilt was stunning. A large red star hung above the bed. On the wood floor was an old, faded rag rug. A tiny window looked out to the street.

Peach trees had already provided beautiful peaches that summer. We always bought some as soon as the sign PEACHES FOR SALE went up.

Out front, the owners had made a stone beehive

with the date 1776 when the house was built. The beehive is Utah's industrious symbol. It stood for "Working together as a community. Supporting one another," he told me.

An antique tractor sat in front of the waist-high rock wall they had constructed. We had always been so intrigued by the look of this house and wondered what it was all about. The owners were always there doing something to it. We were proud to have it on our street. They called it The Farm House.

Across from the historic house, a construction company had just taken out three old homes. Our homes were up around the bend and were considered the newer part of the neighborhood. The construction company had tractors and large equipment hauling remnants of someone's once-lived-in home, now crushed to the ground and demolished.

May and I watched as they smoothed the dirt and hauled it away. We had no idea what the people were paid for their houses. After all, it was the property that was sought after. They had put up a chain link fence around the area, to keep people out and safe.

Before the houses were demolished, I saw men going into the empty houses and taking wood and parts to the fence. Looters were trespassing until the fence got put up with a big fat padlock. It made the entrance to our neighborhood look so different to have the older houses gone. Maybe even an improvement.

The neighbors all talked amongst themselves, speculating what the three house lots were going to be. Apartments? Condominiums? "Or, it could even be a business complex," someone said.

May said when she used to drive, that corner was always her landmark to know where to turn into our neighborhood. I knew if she walked this far by herself, there was a chance that it would confuse her now since her memory was getting worse.

May's car was covered in dust and dirt even though it had been parked in the garage and hadn't been driven in a long time now. To the side of the car was a pile of unused items. Junk I would call it, and that pile kept growing over the years.

The shelves across the back of the garage had dirty garden gloves, pesticides, and spray cans. Every shelf overflowed with things that would never get used again, but she would never throw them away. A sheet of cardboard lay against the wall, along with a 2x4 piece of wood. Sacks of garbage lay at the bottom of the stairs where she had tossed them but never made it to the garbage can. It smelled sour.

May locked herself out of the house and had come to get me. She wanted to know if her brother had ever given me a key to her house.

I told her no, that he hadn't.

She looked like she didn't believe me.

I sternly said, "No, he didn't."

She didn't remember the code to her garage door opener, and it took her several tries to make it open. When the door opened, I said, "Maybe your brother hid a key in here somewhere."

I looked around at the junk that should have been thrown away years ago.

Where to start looking?

I wondered if he would have hidden a key under the mat in her car. I opened the door and checked; the key was not there. May checked on the other side in the glove compartment, which was stuffed with paper napkins and receipts. The key wasn't there either. We closed the car doors and looked around some more. Then she asked me again if her brother had given me a key. I said, "NO. May, I wouldn't be looking with you if he had."

We went on looking and went over to the metal shelving unit that was piled high with dirty tools. I started moving things wishing I had put gloves on. The stench in the garage was starting to make me feel nauseous. May was standing there looking at me.

I asked her if she had checked the door that went into her washroom to see if it was unlocked because I knew she had checked the front door first. I walked up the wooden stairs to check it. It was locked as well. I told her that we keep a key hidden outside for this very reason.

She didn't say anything. She was frustrated. I knew that if Paul could get the go-ahead to clean out this garage, he would hire a dumpster and get rid of all the junk, except her lawn mower. Paul never could understand people that would pile junk up inside their garage, not allowing them to park their cars inside and use the garage for what it was intended for.

I looked at May, she was in a daze. She hadn't brought her phone out with her, but I said, "May, use my phone and call your brother."

"I don't know his number," she said.

"I have it in my contacts."

She looked at me surprised as if she didn't trust me. "Why do you have my brother's phone number?"

I didn't ever tell her that her brother and I occasionally talked about what was going on with her and her memory problems. I got my phone out of my back pocket and found the number. I knew that she wouldn't be able to search for his contact information on her own, so I pushed CALL and handed it to her.

His voicemail came on, so she hung up. She started to hand the phone back to me, and I said, "You should have left a message to tell him what's going on, so he wouldn't think it was me calling him."

She stared at me with an accusing expression on her face. I wasn't going to indulge her. I knew the reasons why we had talked to one another. For the good of May nothing else.

The garage was heating up now, and the open bags of lawn fertilizer smell was permeating the air. I took my phone away from her and called him again. I quickly handed it back to May when it rang.

This time he answered. In her timid voice, she said, "I locked myself out of the house again. Marcelina's here with me."

I could tell that she was embarrassed to have to call him because it had happened many times before. He told her that there was a key tied to a string but didn't say where and hung up before I could take the phone away and get more precise instructions.

I looked at all the walls, looking for a nail with a string tied to it. Screens were hanging from hooks, but no visible sign of a key. I didn't want to have to call him back, so I drilled May.

"What exactly did he say?" She looked numb. After searching all the shelves and rubbing a hand across my sweaty forehead, I was just about to call him back out of exhaustion, when I looked under the wooden stairs.

There discreetly hidden was a key hanging on a string from a nail that was pounded into the wood. I maneuvered my way past her shop vac and the old kitchen chairs that cluttered the way. I retrieved the key and handed it to May. She walked up the three wooden stairs and unlocked the door. She sighed with relief.

She was about to go in when I said, "May, let's put the key back where it was."

She said, "No, I'll put it in my kitchen drawer," not understanding that if she got locked out again, the key would be inside, instead of outside where it needed to be. I worried that the day would come when she wouldn't be able to remember her garage door code at all, even though it was 1234. It was essential that she put the key back where it was because she would most certainly lock herself out again. She was inside, that's all I cared about for now.

I needed a shower.

I woke up to the rumbling of the bedroom shutters. I knew immediately what it was. We were having an earthquake. I jumped out of bed, grabbed my robe, and ran down the hall. The door from the basement flew open almost hitting me in the face.

My son, who had been living with us for a short

time was coming up the stairs. "Are we having an earthquake?"

His dad was sitting in his normal reading chair with the dog on his lap.

"Yes!" He said while I watched the chandelier swing back and forth.

The china in the hutch was clanging, and I looked up at the ceiling fan. I didn't want to stand under there in case it fell.

We all gathered together in our family room, feeling scared, and not sure how long it would last. I made us some coffee while Paul turned on the TV, making sure it was a local news station to see what they were saying about the earthquake.

I thought about May being over there by herself, wondering if she could have possibly slept through it. The news said that there would be aftershocks to follow. I decided to call her because I knew if she had woken up, she would be afraid. I wanted to make sure that she was okay.

She picked up on the first ring.

"Hi, it's me, are you okay?"

She sounded out of breath. "I tried to call my brother, but he didn't answer."

"Do you want to come over to be with us? The news said that there is going to be aftershocks."

She immediately said, "Yes."

Paul and I were still in our robes when she came over. We poured her a cup of coffee We watched the television listening to reports of damage.

I watched as the stiff nervous May relaxed, but then the house started shaking again.

It was worse than the first one. My shoulders tensed up, and I looked over at May who looked even more frightened.

The news reported that buildings had crumbled in one of the smaller towns west of us. So far, nobody had been injured.

Our son, who had been watching with us, went downstairs to get ready to go to work at the university hoping for no damage there.

Paul asked us if we wanted some breakfast. I really didn't feel like eating, but he began getting the eggs and bacon out of the fridge.

May and I sat glued to the TV. When breakfast was ready, we sat in the dining room. I was refilling our coffees when the rumbling started again. The hanging light over the dining room table started to sway. I heard Paul say, "Whoa!"

We all held still as if that would lessen the shaking. I wondered how many more of these aftershocks were we going to have to experience. May and I cleared the table off, and I loaded the dishwasher. Barkley walked over to the door to let me know that he needed to go potty.

"I'm going to take the dog out."

May followed, "I'll go out with you, and go home to see if my brother's called me back yet."

I told her that if she needed to come back over later, she was welcome to. We were staying home all day.

The aftershocks continued throughout the week. Some of them were not even noticeable but picked up on the seismograph, and the news would exaggerate the stories. They would show pictures of the same crumbled building.

When I was in school, they always told us that we lived on a fault line and that someday we would get the "Big One!" The schools in our state still had the Great Shake Out where they practice safety in case of an emergency such as an earthquake. I remembered taking part in that program and hiding under my desk. A 5.9 earthquake was all I had ever been through and hoped that I wouldn't be around when the "Big One" hit.

CHAPTER TWELVE

As we became closer friends, May and I talked about Japanese traditions, and I became more interested in her culture. I could see how important it was to her, and I encouraged her to be proud of her ethnicity. I learned to respect the richness of her heritage.

She started telling the neighbors that she was going to Japan for the third or fourth time and that she still had relatives there, so they were planning a trip. I didn't know if that was true or not.

I read the book *Hotel on the Corner of Bitter and Sweet* by Jamie Ford. Also, *Shanghai Girls* and *Snow Flower and The Secret Fan*, by Lisa See. I always looked for new books by these Chinese American authors.

May couldn't concentrate enough to read a full novel, so I would tell her about each of them when we walked.

May talked about how people couldn't recognize the difference between a Chinese person and a Japanese person. She explained to me the name difference. Chinese names were usually short like Chen, while Japanese names were longer like Takahashi.

If an Asian athlete was competing on TV, May would watch. The sport didn't matter; a golfer, a gymnast, or the rare Asian basketball player like Yuma Watanabe that plays for the Toronto Raptors, or Rui Hachimura that plays for the Washington Wizards. She felt a connection to them because of their ethnicity.

The park where May and I walked was not far from the high school. Teenagers would smoke while hiding in the tree-lined path.

We could smell it, but we ignored it and walked right past them. Some of the kids would sit on the lawn and eat their lunch while their phones blasted rap music. We talked about the disgusting language that came out of their mouths.

The white vinyl fence that backed up to the nicer condos was splattered with graffiti, gang signs, and symbols that we didn't understand. We felt bad about the damage that was done overnight in the park.

Usually, a few days later, the parks and recreation department would spray over it. When the sun went down, eventually the hellions would come out again.

It seemed as if the same kids were always hanging out in the park.

I said to May, "Where are the truancy officers, or is that an old-fashioned term?" I thought they worked closely with the local law enforcement to make sure the kids were in school where they belonged, and where their parents believed that they were.

May and I talked as we walked about how we were taught respect for property, and how we would have *never* skipped school.

"If we'd been caught, we would have gotten a swatting across our butts or worse."

We laughed, and I said, "My mother was not someone you wanted to make angry. My parents cared a lot about what other people thought of their kids and raised us to follow the straight and narrow or else."

May said, her father was the disciplinarian in her family and a very strict authoritarian.

We agreed kids needed more of that these days; to know what their parents expected of them. We felt like our old-school ways were the better ways of raising kids.

"Our family was close, but we were all different in our own ways."

Paul and I had taught our kids love and compassion, and we were there for one another. Not to say we didn't go through trying times, we did. But we went through them together because we loved each other unconditionally.

We weren't perfect, but what was perfect anyway? I knew many people who seemed to think they were perfect. I learned not to judge and to forgive from my mother. She had a hard life growing up.

I told May about my mom's family and how she met my dad.

My mom's dad was an alcoholic, and there was abuse in her home. Women stayed with their abusive husbands back then. They were a poor family living in the country outside of Ames, Iowa.

Her dad was a mean son of a bitch; even when he was sober. Always yelling that the damn kids were always underfoot. There were five siblings from two years old up to fifteen years old.

They were a farming family, but things hadn't been going very well. The drought had made it difficult for her dad to raise the crops that his daddy used to raise, and he felt like a failure.

His wife couldn't work because she had five kids she had to tend to, washing, ironing, and making dinners, with what little she had to work with. Some days she sent one of the younger kids down the road to the Monastery, where the monks would give them their leftover scraps.

The older boys wouldn't be caught dead taking handouts. They were in the fields helping their dad cut the hay. They hated their dad because they had witnessed the abuse he inflicted on their mother. When they tried to step in to protect her, he would turn on them, breaking bones and blackening eyes.

Those boys were afraid of their dad, but the thing they hated the most was that he was a bigot. He hated anybody that was not white like him. When he was drunk, all he yelled about was how the Mexicans were going to take over the crop growing. He was mad that his fellow farmers down the road were hiring migrant workers to help them with the land, and that made him furious.

He knew that he was falling behind because he wouldn't hire anyone to help. A black man stopped by one day looking for good honest work, but he hated how blacks wanted jobs that belonged to white people. There was no way that he was going to hire him, no matter how badly he needed the help.

Instead, he took his thirteen- and fourteen-year-old boys out of school to work in the fields. The boys looked young because they were so scrawny, just like their dad's garden. After spending most of his day in the fields, he couldn't wait to go inside and help himself to the whiskey.

He would sit and stew about the Mexican people

that he said were taking over the cropping. If his wife tried to tell him that was not true, he would back-hand her and tell her to shut the hell up! He would yell at the kids, to go to their rooms.

Dorothy was fifteen years old. She would take her two-year-old sister and go to her room, where she would sing to her to drown out the fighting that was going on downstairs. The boys would head outside for fear he would turn on them after he was done beating on their mother.

They felt like cowards leaving their mother to fend for herself. In their frustration and rage, they cursed him and kicked the dirt. But they didn't want any more broken bones. He was still too strong for them to take on, even in a drunken stupor.

The school that Dorothy attended had various eth-nic students that were her friends. She never brought anyone home. She was embarrassed by her house which needed painting on the outside, the fence that needed fixing, and the broken bikes and toys laying on the front lawn that was mostly weeds and dirt.

She never wanted her friends to meet her intox-icated father, whose drunken appearance was ev-ident with his ruddy complexion and the broken veins on his face. He always had on his sloppy work clothes. The bottom of his pant legs was always caked with mud.

Her mother had been a nice-looking woman at one time, but now after having baby after baby, she had let herself go.

On the nights that he would get physical with her, he would call her names and tell her that she was weak. She would cower to him, trying to keep him from abusing the kids.

He ranted and raved about how nobody helped him, and that was why he couldn't make it in the farming industry. "Those damn Mexicans," he would mumble, slurring his words.

That night she waited until after he passed out. Dorothy's mother was crying. She told Dorothy to leave, to run away.

"I've made arrangements for you to stay with an old friend of mine in Utah, but you have to get there," she said. She dug in her old, rusted coffee can, where she hid money from her drunken husband.

She looked over at the couch where he had passed out to make sure he was still sleeping. She pulled some cash out of the can and handed it to Dorothy.

"Here, go pack a bag and take the next bus out of town. Just get out of here while you can. Hurry up before your dad wakes up."

Dorothy did as she was told. She was so frightened to leave on her own. She didn't know the people she was to meet in Utah, or even how to get there. Her mom handed her a small note with a phone number on it.

"Call this number when you get there."

They hugged, and they were both crying.

"Go!" her mother said, pushing her out the broken screen door.

Dorothy walked as fast as she could down the dirt road that led to town. She didn't know the bus routes or where to start, so she decided to take the first bus that was heading west.

She paid for her ticket and stuffed her small coin purse deep into her coat pocket. It was dark outside, and she felt so alone. When she boarded the Greyhound bus, she tried not to make eye contact with anyone.

She was terrified. The tension and fear she had experienced the last hour made her body shiver involuntarily. Once she was settled in her seat, she pulled her thin coat around her trying to keep warm. She wished the bus would hurry and pull away before her dad caught her, or someone recognized her.

Dorothy never had the money for cosmetics or nice clothes, but she was naturally a pretty girl. Her family usually did their shopping at the local thrift store.

She wanted a better life than what her parents had. She had made up her mind she would not marry someone poor. She'd had enough of that.

Never able to go to a dentist or a doctor when her family needed one. They had almost lost little Louisa, because of that.

She thought about Christmas and how there was nothing under their barren tree that they had cut down from the back of the house. The little ones didn't know any different, but Dorothy and her brothers did.

They heard and saw what other families got for Christmas, but her dad would drink himself into a stupor. One year, he knocked down their modest little Christmas tree scaring the little ones and making them cry.

Dorothy tried to work at the town's coffee shop a few days a week to help out, but her pop told her he didn't want her working where men could ogle at her all day while she was serving.

She hated that her dad made her stay home. She hated her life, and she told her mother so.

The bus wound its way through the countryside, and she thought of her younger siblings that she had left behind. She couldn't help but worry about their welfare. She hoped that the older boys would somehow take care of themselves and not let their dad hurt them anymore.

The bus was headed to Fremont, Nebraska, for its first stop. Dorothy watched out the window as they passed places she hoped she would never see again.

She didn't know what her future held. A lump formed in her throat from the uncertainty she felt.

She leaned against the cool window and soon fell into an exhausted sleep.

It was still dark outside when they arrived at the next town. She heard the bus come to a stop, and new passengers got on.

She turned her face away from the window and put a scarf over her head, trying to disguise herself, in case anyone was following her. The bus started up again with the new passengers.

The new arrivals shuffled back to find empty seats. A young mother and her little girl sat down across from Dorothy. She exchanged pleasantries with the lady who held the child against her chest, and she fell to sleep.

It made Dorothy think of her little sister and how she would miss Dorothy singing to her. She couldn't understand why her mother had put up with the abuse all those years; how she hid what was going on in their home, and the kids were all too afraid to tell anyone.

But this was Dorothy's chance to have a different life, and she sure as hell was going to take it.

The bus drove all night and into the early morning before it stopped in Lincoln Nebraska. This time, three servicemen got on, all decked out in their uniforms. They stumbled down the aisle past Dorothy, just as she took off her scarf.

They must have been on leave partying all night because they reeked of alcohol. Once they were seated, the serviceman on the end turned around.

"Where you headed to sweetheart?" he said in his Southern drawl.

Dorothy ignored him but her face turned red, and the lady across from her looked up.

His buddies laughed, and one of them said, "She doesn't like you."

He pulled a black flask out of his jacket. "You old enough to drink, sweetheart?"

He held the flask up for everyone to see.

She wished they would shut up, and finally said, "I don't drink!"

The young mother across from her smiled.

The men cajoled and carried on loudly for about an hour before the driver threatened to throw them off the bus if they didn't mind their own business and leave the passengers alone.

An hour later, they fell asleep in a drunken slumber. Dorothy was grateful. She had seen enough of that at home.

Now every stop the bus made, she was afraid they would wake up and harass her again. She was glad that she had the lady and her little girl across from her, even though they offered no protection.

Dorothy was starting to get hungry, and her stomach growled loudly. She held her hand over her stomach to hopefully stifle the sound.

The lady looked over at her. She dug into her purse and brought out a plastic bag that held crackers and cheese. She offered some to Dorothy, who gladly accepted it, and she thanked her.

The woman fed some to her little girl who was now awake.

Dorothy was so thankful to have something to eat. She had left her house so fast; she didn't have time to think about food.

Dorothy told the woman her name, but she did not offer her last name.

"I'm Louise Hansen, and this is Emma. We're going to visit Grandma and Grandpa aren't we, Emma? My husband is deployed, and we're going to stay with his parents while he's gone."

Emma kept chewing on her cracker and looked around. Dorothy didn't say where she was from, or where she was going. It was nice to have someone to chat with.

Dorothy was tired of sitting and wanted to get up. She didn't want to walk past the servicemen who hassled her last night, so she asked Louise if she would watch her bag, and she went to the bathroom at the back of the bus.

Once she was inside the bathroom, she locked the door and looked in the mirror. She looked tired. Before she left, she washed her hands and her face. It made her feel better.

She made it back to her seat, when Louise asked, "Do you mind holding Emma while I go now?"

Emma reached for Dorothy. It surprised her and made her feel good. It felt natural to have that little body hang on to her. Without thinking, she began to sing the same song she used to sing to her little sister.

She could feel Emma's little body mold against her, her curly blonde head on Dorothy's shoulder. Emma lifted her head and looked up at Dorothy. She sank back down, content to lay still and listen.

When Louise came back, she reached for Emma, but she wouldn't go. Louise sat down, and Dorothy continued singing.

"You have a beautiful voice."

"Thank you." She was going to say that she used to sing to her little sister but thought better of it. She didn't want to give too much information about herself.

They had been traveling for about a day and a half. The bus driver announced he was going to take a break and stop at a café outside of Cheyenne, Wyoming.

Dorothy wondered if she should get off the bus in case someone recognized her, or if her dad had even reported her missing. She didn't feel good about staying on the bus alone.

Once the bus parked outside the El Rancho Motel and Café, everyone headed off the bus, glad to be able to stand up.

"Careful, don't trip," said the bus driver as he assisted everyone down the stairs. The café was like any other greasy spoon café. The smell of cooked bacon filled the air. The passengers quickly filled up the barstools at the counter, but Dorothy stood at the entrance, not sure where to sit.

Louise Hansen was at the back of the restaurant with Emma and waved at Dorothy. Relieved, she joined them. They both ordered bacon and eggs, a short stack of pancakes, and a glass of orange juice.

Dorothy was so thirsty. She hadn't had any water, and she instantly gulped down the entire glass.

The waitress was a heavy, bosomy gal. She brought their plates, refilled their glasses, and moved on to the next table. No nonsense there. She knew that the passengers were on a timetable to get back to their bus.

The food tasted so good. Even Emma ate bites of pancake with its sweet syrup dripping from her chin.

Mrs. Hansen talked about her husband, how much she missed him, and how she felt so lucky to have his parents to stay with.

Dorothy was careful not to disclose that she was running from an abusive, bigoted father. She said that she was on her way to stay with an aunt, who just had twins, and she was going to nanny for them. She thought that sounded realistic. She felt bad lying, but she couldn't take the chance of anyone overhearing her real circumstances.

They finished their breakfast and headed up to the cash register near the door to pay their bill.

One of the servicemen held the door open for them and smiled as they passed him.

"I'm sorry that my friend was so obnoxious last night," he said. "He was drunk." Dorothy didn't respond. She just wanted to be left alone. She headed straight for the bus, never looking back.

Once they were settled inside, with their bellies full, she knew she would rest some more. They still had a way to go, before they reached Utah. She felt like they were far enough away now, that she didn't have to worry.

As soon as Emma settled down in her mama's arms and closed her eyes, Dorothy felt the heaviness of her own eyelids. The bus passed a field of migrants working hard in the sun.

If my dad hadn't been such a racist, he could have hired some of them to work alongside him, maybe his fields would have flourished.

But he was still an alcoholic, too proud to ask for help.

Dorothy fell into a much-needed deep sleep.

She didn't wake up until they stopped again to let passengers off and new ones get on.

Louise stood. "This is our stop, Emma."

Dorothy had been dreading this time when she would be alone. They hugged goodbye, and she watch as they exited the bus. Out the window, she watched them meet up with Emma's grandparents. The love was so apparent, and the happiness they showed on their faces at seeing Emma was so heart-warming. Emma didn't reach out to them as she did with Dorothy.

The grandpa picked up their bags and led them to his car. She was sure she would never see them again. A tear rolled down her face as she watched them drive away.

She was tired of being on the bus and trying to figure out her route to get to Utah. She had never traveled so far from home. She didn't recognize the names of most of the towns that they had stopped at. She closed her eyes and pictured the map that had been posted on the wall in her social studies classroom at her school, trying to remember which state came next.

Maybe I should just get off the bus and stay in a hotel.

After all, she had been traveling for two days now, and her bottom was getting numb from all the sitting. She decided that at the next stop, she would get off the bus and find a pay phone to call her mom.

Would that be safe, she wondered? Had her dad been searching for her? She prayed that he hadn't beaten the truth out of her mom.

"Just one less mouth to feed," he would probably say.

She doubted that he had even contacted the sheriff about her running away. The kids at school would wonder why she wasn't there.

She sometimes went to school with bruises from trying to pry her brothers off their daddy, while he was beating on their mama.

The older kids always got beat on, but the younger ones were just as traumatized by what they had to witness.

Thinking about all that gave her a headache and a knot in her stomach.

The bus stopped, and she saw the sign that said, "Welcome to Cheyenne, Wyoming."

She got off the bus with her one bag and the small purse she kept close because it held the pitiful amount of money that her mama had given her.

She looked down the road to see if she could see a hotel to stay at. She walked past a couple of shops and a shoe store, where she crossed the street when she saw a vacancy sign. She went to the office and inquired about renting a room.

The man at the desk said, "You look a little young to be on your own, missy."

She replied, thinking of Mrs. Hansen and Emma, and said, "Oh, I'm not alone, my husband has nights leave from the Army, and he's coming to meet me."

The desk clerk smiled and said, "We appreciate those boys that risk their lives for our country. My best to you two."

He handed her a key and said, "Room 201."

Dorothy immediately headed up the stairs with her bag. She opened the door to her room and went inside. Her whole body collapsed on the bed, and she began sobbing. What was she doing? She felt so alone and frightened.

She hoped that her dad wouldn't find out that her mother had anything to do with her leaving, or he'd beat the hell out of her. She hoped that her mom would play dumb.

Dorothy needed this stay at the hotel but knew she couldn't afford another night. She had the money for the bus, a couple of meals, and then it would be gone. It had felt so good to sleep in a bed, have a bath, and wash her hair. Time was getting close to where she would be staying with people she had never met before. Could she do this?

After a few more hours on the bus and she finally arrived at her destination. She called the phone number that her mom had written on the piece of paper and told her who she was and that she was at the bus terminal.

The woman said, "I will be there in twenty minutes," and hung up without saying who she was, and how she knew Dorothy's mother.

Dorothy looked around; she had never been here before. Was this a big city? She didn't know. It was definitely different from where she came from. It was called Salt Lake City.

When the woman finally showed up, she apologized for being late, explaining she had to pick her kids up from school before she left. Dorothy was surprised to see that her mother's friend was Hispanic. Did her dad know about this friend of her mom's? Dorothy thanked her for picking her up.

"I'm Ester. I knew your mom in school before she met your dad."

That answered everything.

Ester had lived in Iowa when she was young, and her dad had heard there was work in Utah, so he packed his family up and moved there. She said that it was hard to leave her best friend. As they got older, Dorothy's mom would write to Ester to keep in touch. It was her senior year in school when Dorothy's mother got pregnant and was forced to get married. She knew her boyfriend could be violent at times, but he never touched her while she was pregnant.

They took over the family farm, and then she wrote and told Ester how miserable her life was.

"I tried to talk her into leaving after you were born," she said, "but she was too afraid to leave, and then it got harder as more babies came."

Dorothy cried while Ester told her everything she knew.

"I couldn't come and get her. Your dad was such a bigot, he would have killed me, much less let me in your house. He hated me and wouldn't let your mother come to see me. I remember the phone call from the grocery store in town where your mother called from.

"She had sneaked away and called me and said that his abuse had gone from her to you kids. I told her to call the sheriff. He had several run-ins with your dad and his drinking. He would spend a night in jail, then they would let him out, and it would happen all over again."

Dorothy was ashamed that Ester knew what her mom's life had become.

It was dinner time, and by then Ester's whole family was home. Her eldest son was eighteen and worked at the copper mine. Her next child was a girl named Lottie. She was fifteen years old and had long black braids and the prettiest smile. The third child a boy, six years old, was full of questions.

He wanted to know why she was going to live with them.

"We'll talk about it later, let's get dinner on the table," said Ester.

Her husband Ricardo welcomed Dorothy into their home and told her that they would do anything they could to make her feel comfortable. Everyone was so nice to her; she couldn't believe it.

Ester set the tamales on the table, and Lottie followed with the pinto beans and the tortillas. Ricardo brought the Spanish rice. Everybody bowed their heads to bless the food they were about to eat. Enrique, the eldest son, offered the prayer, making sure he prayed for Dorothy's safety, well aware of her situation.

They were a Catholic family, and Dorothy knew nothing about Catholicism. Everybody started filling their plates as Dorothy watched. She had never had Mexican food before.

She watched as they unwrapped the tamale husk and set it aside. She did the same thing. They poured the beans over the top of the tamale and scooped some of the rice. They all ate so vigorously that she joined right in, thinking it was so different from what she would eat at her house.

She loved the taste of the masa that was wrapped around the pork.

I like tamales.

The Mexican rice had just enough spice in it to not overpower the rest of the food. She watched as Ricardo poured the homemade salsa over his whole plate and began tearing pieces of tortillas to eat the food with, instead of using a fork.

Ricardo noticed she was watching him.

"You can see that Mexicans don't need silverware, as long as we have a tortilla," he said.

Everybody laughed. Ester did the same. Dorothy decided that she would pour a little bit of salsa on her rice, and Lottie told her to be careful because it was hot.

"It's not hot for Mom and Dad, but it might be for you." Lottie was right.

The minute Dorothy put the salsa-covered rice in her mouth, her eyes started to water, and her face turned red. She immediately took a drink of milk. Everybody cracked up.

"You'll get used to it," Lottie said. Dorothy wasn't sure about that.

It turned out to be such a good fit. Dorothy learned to love her new family. They all treated her well and were so nice to her. They each had chores expected of them.

Ester worked full-time at a Mexican restaurant and was a wonderful cook. Ricardo worked at the copper mine and had his son start there after he graduated from high school.

They were thankful to have jobs at the mine, even though they worked out in the elements, at times.

Ester came from a large Hispanic family that had many fiestas for the family to get together. It was always so fun and festive. As far as they were concerned, she was one of the family.

Dorothy started to hang out with the kids from the Catholic Church they attended. They never made her feel any different than the rest of them, even though most of the people there were Hispanic, and she wasn't.

Dorothy started dating Ester's oldest son, Enrique. He was so handsome. He had wavy black hair and big brown eyes, with the longest black eyelashes. She would tease him saying, "With those kinds of eyelashes you should have been a girl," and he would tell her she was just jealous.

They had been dating for over a year now, and at times she wondered what her dad would think or say about their relationship. Ester and Ricardo on the other hand totally approved of them being together, but Ester did ask the kids to wait to get married until Dorothy had graduated from high school. That would give Enrique time to save some money for their future together.

Dorothy never went back home again, and two years later, she married Enrique. She had never been so happy in her whole life.

When her dad found out that she married a Hispanic man, he said that she did it just to defy him, and he told her mother that he never wanted to see her again; that they were not welcome in his home.

Even her mother had said, "I sent you there to protect you, not to get married."

"That's it," Dorothy said to Enrique. "I never want to see any of them again."

Dorothy and Enrique bought a small house in a young neighborhood. Dorothy learned to cook Mexican food and worked hard to be active in their community. Enrique was so proud of his new wife and how she adjusted to his way of living. A year later, Dorothy found out that she was pregnant.

She was so excited and couldn't wait to tell her husband. He was overcome with happiness, and he picked her up off the floor and twirled her around, kissing her face at the same time.

The years went by fast. Enrique worked hard to provide for his family. There were times he experienced discrimination, but he overcame it and worked his way up to be a supervisor at the copper mine. By then, they had four kids. He worked double shifts and all the overtime he could get. They needed more money now because it was time to buy a new house. With four kids, they were bursting at the seams and needed more space.

Dorothy received word from her brother that her dad had been killed in a farming accident. She didn't know how to feel about it. It had been so many years. Did she still hate him?

Her brother asked her if she was going to come to the funeral, and she said, "No, I have four kids to take care of now."

Dorothy learned to forgive her dad as the years went by. She knew that it was an addiction that made him so hard to live with. A person that she had hated his actions, but not him anymore.

She realized after being a parent herself, that her parents did the best they could, and there were definitely some mental health issues there, as well. She never went back home, until her mother was eighty-five years old, in a nursing home in Iowa, and didn't have long to live.

By then Dorothy and Enrique's kids were married and out of their house. Dorothy was honest with her adult children, telling them that she chose the love of her life over her parents that were racist. She thought about what her mother had sacrificed for her to get away and decided to go see her before she passed.

Her middle daughter told her that she would go with Dorothy, after all, she had never met her grandmother. They talked on the airplane about the horrible life Dorothy and her mother had endured, and how sorry she felt for her mother all those years ago.

The bitterness in her heart was gone and was replaced by forgiveness.

I apologized to May for going on and on about my parents, but she seemed so enthralled. She didn't seem to tire of my family stories; in fact, it seemed to encourage her to talk about her upbringing and what it was like.

How was it that we could converse for hours on end, never tiring of listening to one another? It seemed to help her open up her cloudy mind to things she might have forgotten.

Through the years, the more time I spent with May the more we seemed to become alike. I stopped wearing makeup, stopped straightening my hair, and wore it naturally curly. I became very casual.

She taught me to love comfort. I began wearing clogs like her when we were out in the garden together. She still wore athletic T-shirts, and I started wearing tie-dye shirts.

I hadn't worn cutoff shorts since my teen years, and despite the veins in my legs, I started to wear shorts like hers. I felt a sense of freedom from having to dress up. I knew I could just be myself with May. She never thought anything about it. She didn't care about impressing anyone, she was truly herself.

One day, Paul and I took her to Sam's club where she loved to go. She was always saying, "I have a Sam's club card or a Costco card if you ever want to go."

In the past, she would spend a lot of money, but she wanted to go, so I took her.

Sam's had their capris on sale, so we both bought the same ones and decided that we wouldn't wear them on the same day, and then we would laugh. May bought three pairs of shoes, saying that she would save them for next year.

I tried to talk her into getting one pair, but she ignored me and put all three boxes in the basket that we shared. She bought socks and winter pajamas, even though I reminded her that she bought two pairs of pajamas the last time I took her shopping.

She bought large quantities of toilet paper and paper towels. She threw in the lunch meats and cheeses that I was sure would just spoil in her refrigerator. Thank goodness a family member eventually cleaned out her fridge. She shopped like she was not going to get back to a store for a long, long time. I felt like she was out of control, but she wouldn't listen to me.

Paul took me aside and said, "We can't bring her to these kinds of stores anymore, Marcelina. Her family is going to be mad at us for letting her buy all this stuff."

I told May we had everything we needed now, and we were ready to go, but she wanted to keep shopping. She said, "Just let me look at these pots and pans."

I looked at Paul. "Why would she need pots and pans, she doesn't even cook."

Paul shrugged his shoulders.

"May, let's look at those next time we come." I steered the cart toward the checkout.

CHAPTER THIRTEEN

....

*P*AUL AND I had just returned from our Panama Canal cruise, and I couldn't wait to tell May about the sights we had seen on our trip. Even though May had traveled a lot, she had never been on a cruise.

I repeatedly told her how much fun Paul and I had, and how I loved to cruise. We had a group of friends we called, our "traveling buddies." We all got along well. Each friend had a unique personality that added to the fun that we had. We had been to Alaska, Europe, the Caribbean, and now the Panama Canal.

May asked, "Which one was your favorite?"

"I can't choose a favorite. I enjoyed them all."

I brought May a coffee mug from each place we went. It always made her so happy.

We asked her to bring our mail in for us while we were gone. We knew we were taking a chance she might get it mixed up with hers.

We had been gone for sixteen days, but I could have stayed longer. As it turned out, it was good we came home when we did because COVID-19 Pandemic broke out.

It was all over the news. Cruise ships were stranded at sea with passengers deathly sick with it. We were so thankful that we weren't on one of those ships. Every day, May and I were stunned to see the number of people who were getting sick and dying.

We decided together that we were going to do what the CDC suggested to keep from getting it. We stayed home, not wanting to be around other people who may or may not have it.

May was at my house, or I was at hers. We waited for months and months for a vaccine.

Paul invited May to have lunch with us. I mentioned to her that if she ever got COVID-19, most likely I would get it, and vice versa, because we were together almost every day, but Paul and I hadn't even been around our kids or grandkids for fear of getting it. We decided we were only going to go to the store when it was absolutely necessary.

May came over to hang out with Paul and me and said, "Did you see on the news how many people have Covid now?"

She sat down on the floor to pet Barkley. "Yes, I did."

I set a bowl of miniature candy bars on the coffee table, and she surprised me when she said, "Do you remember buying penny candy when you were young?"

"I do, we always bought it from a little market called Arnie's. It was so hard to look through the glass case and try to decide what to get."

"Remember rotary telephones that hung on our walls? Some people had party lines, where if you were quiet enough, you could listen to their conversations. I would listen to my oldest sister talk to her boyfriend," I admitted.

"Marcelina!"

Paul could hear us talking, and he added, "Remember when Coke was in the green bottles that you could get out of a machine? My friends and I would go looking for bottles that people would toss away. We collected as many as we could to redeem, so we could buy a large-size Coke. We would drink it on the way home, seeing who could burp the loudest."

May and I laughed. She said she couldn't picture Paul ever doing something like that.

I was an avid reader after I retired. The first thing after waking up and pouring myself a cup of coffee, I would sit down to read. Paul would already be up and well engrossed in his book. I loved that quiet time set aside for reading before I went out for my walk.

Because I liked it so much, I tried to encourage May to read. I thought it would be good for her brain. When we went shopping together, she would buy three or four books, usually all Danielle Steel.

I didn't think those books would ever get read, she just couldn't concentrate.

I would tell her, "May, you can't read with the television on. You need to shut the TV off, so you can concentrate." But eventually, the books would get lost in the clutter, until she would shop again to buy more and add to her unread book cemetery.

Once after May had been at my house when I had a vanilla candle burning, she brought out some old candles that she found.

She asked me, "Where do you buy your candles from?"

I told her, "The bath and body store."

She showed me her old, faded candles with no lids that had never been burned, and there was no smell left. She said she wasn't sure if she had any matches.

I could have easily offered to bring some over to her but knew it was not a good idea. It all made me really uncomfortable because I didn't think with her memory problem, she should be burning candles. Instead, I talked her into setting them on the glass plant stand by her front window in the sun. I told her that as the sun heated the wax, maybe some of the aromas would be released. I made that up, but she seemed to believe me, and said, "That's a good idea."

May set them down as I had suggested. I hoped like hell she wouldn't look for matches after I was gone.

It was three o'clock in the morning when I heard Barkley barking at the door wanting to go outside. I waited to see if Paul would rouse to take him out. I lay there listening, as his soft snoring continued.

Damn, he wasn't getting up. I put my robe and slippers on and went to the front door where he was patiently waiting to go potty. It was pitch black outside, except for the bright moon shining.

I carefully walked down the front porch steps. Barkley had night blindness now, so I gave him time to find each step. When we both reached the bottom of the stairs, he immediately ran onto the lawn to sniff around until he found the perfect spot to do his business. I waited patiently, looking up and down our street at the dark houses in the crisp night air.

It always gave me an eerie feeling to be outside at this time of the night. I had always thought that anybody that was out at this time of the night was up to no good. Just as Barkley had finished going potty, and I was reeling him in on his leash, I looked left in front of May's house, and there stood a man dressed all in black, including a black beanie hat, with a black backpack on.

I froze.

I could feel my heart racing, so I held still, thinking if I didn't move, maybe he wouldn't see me. I hoped that Barkley wouldn't bark and give us away.

The man was on the sidewalk just past our trailer, looking at May's dark house. I wanted to see what he was up to even though I was scared. I thought, if he comes toward me, I'll scream as loud as I can, and run up the stairs. Despite Barkley's night blindness, he would realize something was wrong and would hopefully go nuts.

I had to make sure that the man wasn't going to go into May's house, so I stood there in fear and waited. Considering how he was dressed, he probably didn't want to be seen.

I wished that I had my cell phone, so then I could call my son-in-law who was a police officer. However, he hadn't done anything wrong that I could tell.

Was it someone that knew that she lived all alone? Who maybe had been watching her? I had confided in a few of the neighbors that she had been diagnosed with Alzheimer's, not to gossip, but to let them know so that they could help me keep a watch out for her in case she was confused or lost.

Those few seconds that I stood there felt like forever.

All of a sudden, I realized he saw me. My heart pounded. I knew if he got closer, Barkley would see him.

I wanted to yell out "get the hell out of here, or I'm calling the police!" But I couldn't speak. He immediately started walking really fast, and whatever was in his backpack was clanging around. It sounded like metal. He hurried past my house, not looking my way on purpose.

I brought Barkley inside, took his leash off, and went straight to the front bedroom to look out the window. I searched up and down the street, looking for any movement. I was nervous, but I couldn't see anything. I wondered if May had seen anything. She sometimes wanders around her house at night when she can't sleep. I didn't want to alert her since he was gone, but an uneasiness stayed with me.

I went to our bathroom window that faced the side of May's house. No lights on, and everything was dark inside. No sign of her being up. I thought about waking Paul up to tell him what had happened but thought better of it, after seeing Barkley already snuggled up against him, back to sleep.

I walked back into the front room for one last look. Even our neighbors whom we called the "night people" had gone to bed. They usually stayed up until two or three in the morning.

I felt like I needed to protect my friend since she was alone. I laid down on the bed in the front bedroom, so I could periodically look out the shutters and not be in full view. When my nerves finally settled down, I fell asleep. Paul told me when he woke up the next morning, he came out to see if I was possibly on the couch, but I wasn't. Barkley followed him to the front bedroom where I lay sleeping. After he saw me, he quietly closed the bedroom door, allowing me to sleep.

I woke up at ten o'clock in the morning. I had never slept that late before. Paul had wondered if I was sick in the night.

I came out of the bedroom with my blonde hair standing on end and sleepers in my eyes. Paul was sitting at the dining room table using his computer.

"Have a hard night?"

I started telling him about what went on, and how frightened I was for May. "I don't think I went to sleep until early morning."

Paul was very concerned. He stood and went outside, looking for what, I didn't know. I stayed in the house and watched him walk in front of May's house looking at her back gate that appeared to be left open during the night.

He didn't look like he could decide if he should walk back there to check things out or not. He later said he had to make sure. Paul walked through the side gate that led to May's backyard. Luckily, May's blinds were still closed on her glass sliding door. Paul walked around, looking for anything amiss. He checked her deck and her garden tools. Her rake and shovel were leaning up against the house, her dirty gardening gloves in a gray bucket sitting on the patio.

It was then that he heard the patio door unlock, and May stepped out the door. He said she was shocked to see Paul there, and she spilled her coffee. We had decided that we wouldn't mention the man outside her house last night because we knew it would upset her.

Paul said he stammered around, trying to think fast what to say to her. He had to tell her the truth because she caught him in her backyard. He told her to sit down, that he had something to tell her.

She immediately looked worried.

He said, "I'm going to go get Marcelina first, so she can tell you why I'm looking around."

Paul came and got me, and I angrily said, "I thought we weren't going to tell her?"

"I had no choice. She saw me looking around."

We were only trying to protect her. She was such a nervous little thing as it was. We walked to the backyard where she was sitting. She looked up at me like she was wondering what was going on.

I sat across from her and told her word for word what I had experienced last night. I explained how I was not going to go back to bed until I was sure that she was not in any danger but reassured her that he was gone out of our neighborhood.

She asked me, "Why didn't you get Paul up?"

"I didn't want to lose sight of him."

"Did he come into my backyard?" she asked Paul, rather than me.

"I don't know. Your gate was open, that's why I was checking things out. Maybe he was thinking about coming back here until he saw Marcelina."

I saw May's body shudder, as she took a sip of her coffee.

"Should I call the police?"

"There doesn't seem to be any reason to call now," said Paul. "He didn't seem to do anything wrong."

"He just looked intimidating, dressed all in black and out at three o'clock in the morning. I just didn't like the way he stopped in front of your house and was looking at it," I said.

"Maybe because your side gate was left open, which we didn't know about until this morning," Paul added.

"I'm going to talk to my brother about getting outside security cameras," said May.

I remembered that she had visited that idea with him before, and he didn't think a security system would work for her. The way she wandered at night, it would always be going off.

"We didn't mean to scare you, May, but we all need to keep a lookout now since we don't know what he was up to."

I tried to lighten the conversation by asking her if she had seen the movie, *Our Souls at Night* with Robert Redford and Jane Fonda. In the movie, their characters were both widowed neighbors, not wanting to get remarried. She asks him if he wants to spend the nights with her in her bed, so she didn't have to be alone at night. A platonic friendship. I loved the book and the movie.

She didn't look amused. I thought it was funny, but she failed to see the humor in it. She still looked worried. I knew that she would be on alert now, and so would we.

CHAPTER FOURTEEN

At the end of the street was the path leading to the park we walked in. Trees lined both sides of the trodden, dirt path. The dry canal to the left was strewn with leaves, branches, and garbage.

May and I loved walking through the center of the trees that formed an arched over our heads. The leaves were sparse but were bright green, and the summer sun shone through the branches.

It always concerned May that there wasn't a fence between the path and the canal. She talked about how people could fall in there if they walked too close to the edge. "I can't believe that people throw their garbage in there," she said.

"I'm sure it's the teenage kids that hide out here smoking and drinking beer."

One day, May and I decided we would put our work gloves on and clean up the debris that people so thoughtlessly threw in there.

At the start of the walking path was a playground where we could watch the little kids on the playground equipment, a baseball diamond, and the county had planted beautiful canna lilies all around the water fountain. We felt so lucky to have this beautiful place to walk.

It was so good for May to get outside and be away from the TV to open up her mind and talk to another living person, instead of just the telephone which had become her way of life.

Once when we rounded the corner past the water fountain, a toddler and other young kids were screaming with laughter as they slid down the slide and climbed onto the tricky bars.

It thrilled May to see the little ones having so much fun. If a child ever came close to the walking track, May would always stop and talk to them. She seemed to love little kids so much. It made me wonder why she never married and had kids of her own. Was it that she had to take care of her mother after her dad died or were there other reasons that I was unaware of, even as close as we were?

That was a subject that she didn't discuss for any length of time. My curiosity was getting the best of me, but I didn't want to ruin our friendship by making her talk about something that made her uncomfortable.

Maybe she couldn't remember. I had certainly opened up to her about things that were near and dear to my heart, knowing she wouldn't judge me. I loved that about her. An unlikely friendship had flourished through the years.

I tried to make sure that I saw her at least once a day to make sure she was okay. She was alone in her house. I didn't want something to happen to her, and no one would know about it for days.

When Barkley and I would go to pick her up to walk, if she didn't answer the door, it would always concern me. I hated to be a pest if she didn't want to be bothered, but more than the walking, I wanted to make sure she was all right.

I felt bad that she was by herself all day. I knew she was lonely. I told Paul that I had read an article that said, loneliness made people two times more likely to get dementia. "Loneliness can definitely affect a person's mental health which can cause cognitive decline," I said.

I went on to tell him that as a person gets older and has seen the effects of Alzheimer's on people they know, they worry when they can't think of names or when they go into a room to get something and can't remember what they went there for.

"We all have senior moments. You've heard our friends attest to that," said Paul.

"But when is it time to be concerned about someone forgetting things? Do you think if our kids notice when we struggle to remember a word, or we repeat the same stories, not remembering that we've told them before? Will they let us know? How much of that is normal?"

"Marcelina," Paul said, "you're getting out of control. We don't have Alzheimer's." He stood, put his arms around me, and said, "I'll tell you if you start acting like May."

"Paul, don't say that it's not funny. I feel so sorry for her." I started to cry.

I so appreciated having a husband to kiss good morning and good night. Someone to talk to, to share my thoughts with; someone to cuddle with and make me feel content.

May didn't have that. She was alone day in and day out. No one to discuss the news with, no one to complain to about her aches and pains. No one to make her feel loved. I wondered if she had ever felt love, other than from her family. She had never mentioned it to me.

She had told me about a Japanese man who she bowled with. He lived in Hawaii now. She would show me the box he sent her every Christmas that was filled with goodies. It seemed to mean a lot to her. Was he more than a friend? I think she would have told me, and he was married and had kids anyway.

As time went on, May really couldn't do much of anything on her own but stay home in her house. I wondered about her Japanese friends. Where were those *good* friends now? Why aren't they coming to see her? Take her places? Do things to help her?

I was mad at them and didn't even know who they were. It was hard on her that she couldn't do the things she used to do. She took care of her mother, mowed her lawn, cleaned her own house, paid her bills, gassed up her car, and kept up with repairs so that she could get to her job.

Now, she wasn't able to do any of that.

That summer, we were getting ready for our next camping trip. I asked May if she had ever been camping.

"Yes, in a tent with my brothers."

"Camping in a trailer is totally different than roughing it in a tent. Would you want to go with us in our trailer?"

She wasn't so sure. She said that she would think about it.

I told Paul that I asked May to go camping with us, and he wasn't very happy with me for doing that.

He said, "We're going to have to watch her like a hawk."

"That's ok, it'll be good for her. I'll take full responsibility for her if she decides to go."

May never said anything about going with us, so I thought she had decided not to, until the day before we were going to leave. We were out packing the trailer when she quietly peeked her head through the trailer door and said, "Am I still invited to go?"

I turned around from stacking some can goods on a shelf and said, "Sure you are."

Paul just kept unpacking the crate he had brought in, never looking up.

"What should I bring?" she excitedly asked.

"We'll take care of all the food. You just bring your clothes and a pillow. We have plenty of bedding."

The next morning, she was at our door. She looked a little apprehensive but had her bag packed and a pillow under her arm. I told her we were going to have good weather for all four days that we would be camping.

"Did you call your brother to let him know where you're going?"

"Yes, I called him last night, and he thought that was nice that you're taking me with you. He reminded me to pack my medications that are all lined up in the pill case for the whole week, and to take my cell phone."

The three of us and our dog hopped into our

truck with the trailer hitched up and drove out of our neighborhood. May was staring out the window, and I wondered if she had second thoughts about going, but she didn't say anything.

It took us about two hours to get to the campground where we liked to stay. We had to make reservations almost a year in advance to get in. It was hot in the city, so it would feel nice to go up in the canyons. We liked to camp where there were a lot of trees for plenty of shade.

We weren't desert campers at all.

When we arrived, I told May that there was about an hour's worth of work for Paul to get us set up. He had to unhitch the trailer and level it. He had to get the electricity hooked up, as well as get the sewer and water connected.

I usually just get out of his way, so I decided to take her and Barkley for a walk around the campground. The whole time May was holding on tight to her purse that hung over her shoulder. I tried to get her to leave it in the trailer, but she wouldn't part with it. We both had our walking shoes on, so we went around twice, while I pointed out things that might interest her.

The campground was like a KOA, with a swimming pool and a jacuzzi. It had a little country store that I took her in to look around. They sold essentials that campers might have forgotten, like ketchup, mustard, syrup, pancake mix, and other items that filled the shelves. On the opposite wall were toiletries, shampoo, bar soap, and toilet paper.

Higher up on pegs were things like Advil, Pepto, and Benadryl. They had all kinds of swim toys. Water wings, blowup rafts, and beach balls of many colors.

As we were about to walk out of the store, May spotted an area that had items for sale that were homemade by the local people. They had painted wooden signs with unique sayings on them. There were embroidered dish towels and crocheted scrubbies. We had looked for quite a while at the handmade items when I said, "Let's come back later. I'm sure Paul has everything hooked up by now, and I'll make us some lunch."

We walked back to camp, and Paul was just finishing up disconnecting the truck from the trailer. We went inside and opened up the blinds. It was hot outside, so I turned on the air conditioner.

May just kind of stood there looking around at our miniature house on wheels. I started to pull things out of the small refrigerator and said, "You can sit down and make yourself comfortable."

I put the deli turkey on the table and grabbed a loaf of bread from the overhead cupboard where the potato chips were. I laid them both next to the turkey on the table in front of May. I sliced up some freshly washed tomatoes from our garden and asked May, "Do you like pickles on your sandwich?"

"Yes."

So, I sliced them up and washed some lettuce leaves as well.

May never offered to help with anything. It was as if she was in her own little world. She didn't even converse. I called Paul in to have lunch, and he finally got her to talk. He told her how we had been coming up to this campground since our kids were little.

"They had so much fun here, they could run wild, and we didn't have to worry about them," he said. "They could fish in the pond, follow trails around the campground, swim in the pool, play basketball or horseshoes, but what they really liked was the game room."

I hadn't shown that to May yet. Paul laughed. "They loved that damn thing. They were always asking for quarters. We could always get them to do chores at home, with a promise of earning some quarters. We had some great family time here when our kids were young. Jed and Carol, the owners, took such great pride in the campground. The manicured lawns were fertilized and watered to a fresh green."

Carol kept bright healthy colored petunias in pots

in each corner of the swimming pool area, with a Spike plant in the middle.

"Our kids always loved coming here, and we still do."

He told her about a family that had two boys around the same age as our kids, and we camped with them for years. They all got along so well. After the kids had a full day of running around exploring and swimming for hours, we would all sit around the picnic table and play board games. Everybody's faces would be red from being in the sun. May had never done any of that before. She intently listened to Paul's stories, but I'm not so sure that she could sense the nostalgia that he was conveying in his memories. I added bits and pieces to the conversation while we were eating our lunch. I brought up the time that we put our tired little kids to bed after a long day, and our friends did the same in their trailer parked next to us.

When they thought that their boys were asleep, they sneaked over to our trailer to play cards. Our kids were sound asleep in their bunk beds.

We played a couple of hands of rummy when there was a knock on our trailer door. When Paul opened the door, it was pitch black outside. There stood Jed, the owner of the campground, holding the hand of our friend's youngest son. He had on his footed pajamas and didn't seem afraid at all.

Jed said, "Does this little guy belong to anyone? I found him outside wandering around when I was locking up the gate to the pool area."

Patty jumped up from the table and grabbed him in her arms, hugging him tightly. I explained to Jed that they thought their boys would stay asleep while we played a couple of hands of cards.

"I'm just glad that I saw him instead of someone else, they could have taken him," he sternly said.

We all felt embarrassed and chastised.

Patty and Peter left and went back to their trailer. I cleaned up the table and put the cards away, thinking about how lucky we were that nothing happened to their little boy.

After hearing that story, May's eyebrows furrowed. "Why would they leave their trailer door unlocked with their boys asleep?"

"Times were different then, May, that's the way it was back then. We felt safe here, and they thought their boys would just sleep while they were gone."

It was obvious she didn't think that was a very good decision.

We didn't tell her anymore of our experiences.

I poured us a Diet Coke and ice, and we went outside to sit in our lawn chairs. We watched the stream of trailers that poured into the campground now that school was out, and families were able to load their kids up to get away for the weekend. Huge motor homes passed us coming down the one-way road, waving hello as they went by. We had our books in our laps with every intention of reading, but the parade of campers kept our interest, so we never did open them.

"This is pretty much what we do down here, relax in our folding chairs. We read, walk, and we eat a lot."

"That's nice."

"The couple that we used to camp with sold their trailer and built a cabin, so they don't come up here anymore. Our married kids own a boat, so they head to the lakes to do their own thing with their friends, but we still like coming here to a place that holds so many good memories for us."

While we sat there, Paul reminded me of how he and Peter used to talk about the big rigs that would pass by us, and how much people would spend on their motorhomes and trailers. We were just fine with the comfortable but small travel trailers that we worked hard for.

Nothing was ever given to us. We all worked hard to live the good life we assumed we had. After a long week of working, we always looked forward to our camping trips. We were lucky to have good friends that we could complain about things with.

When I thought she was tired of hearing us reminisce, I decided it was hot enough to go over to the swimming pool.

I said to May, "If you want to go get your swimming suit on, we'll get ours on after you."

She looked surprised. "I didn't bring a swimming suit. I didn't know that there would be a swimming pool at a campground."

"That's okay, it's my fault that I didn't let you know. We can just go over to the pool and watch."

"You two go and swim. I will stay here with Barkley and watch you guys."

I was a little hesitant to do that because of her Alzheimer's, but I knew we could see our campsite from the pool area, so we said okay. We went inside the trailer, got our suits on, grabbed two towels and some cold waters, and left for the pool. While we were walking over there, I could hear Barkley barking, wanting to come with us, and May trying to calm him down.

The swimming pool area was crowded, but mostly with kids. Paul leaned over and said, "I wonder how many of these kids have peed in the pool?" I laughed.

I wasn't thrilled about taking my swimming suit cover-up off and presenting my old body in full view of everyone to see, but I hurried and dropped my towel to the ground and jumped in, enjoying the coolness of the water. I tried not to put my head under the water because of what Paul had said about the kids peeing in the water. Paul joined me. We tried to doggie paddle away from the kids, while floats were knocking into our heads. Kids were screaming "Marco," while other kids yelled back "Polo" in return. It had been about an hour when we decided we'd better get back to May and our dog. We carefully got our drenched bodies out of the pool and dried ourselves off. We put our flip-flops on and headed toward our campsite.

Paul said he couldn't wait to shower, and I said, "Oh a little pee never hurt anybody! We've done this for years, dear."

The closer we got to our campsite, we couldn't see May or Barkley. We thought they had gone inside, but when we reached the trailer and looked, they weren't there. Now I was concerned. We asked the campers next door if they had seen a small Japanese lady with a dog.

They pointed down the trail and said, "It was about an hour ago when we saw her." They said they noticed her because she was almost yanking him away from the campsite, and he didn't want to go. I was so afraid they were lost or had fallen in the river that ran past the campground where people fished.

My heart was beating fast, and I said to Paul, "We never should have left her alone."

We hadn't taken the time to change, so when we headed further down the path, thorny bushes scratched our bare legs.

Sticks were poking me inside my flip-flops, and rocks were throwing me off balance as we walked as fast as we could. We kept searching and listening to hear if we could hear barking.

The falls up ahead were roaring and made it hard to hear anything but the rushing water. The trail went for miles around the large campground. Would she have gone that far by herself? She rarely went outside our neighborhood for fear of getting lost, and not remembering how to get back.

Some cutoffs branched off the main trail. We wondered if she had taken one of those.

"Should we split up?" I asked Paul.

"No!" sounding a little sharper than he intended to, and he knew it. He was just as afraid as I was.

"Let's stay together," he said in a much calmer voice this time. The brush was becoming denser, and less of the path was evident.

We were just about to start yelling her name out loud when I noticed May sitting by a tree holding the dog. He immediately jumped out of her arms, scratching her with his nails.

"Mayumi, there you are! We have been looking for you."

She stood, and we noticed that she had wet herself. She looked so scared.

I hugged her.

"It's ok, I'm glad you stopped and didn't go any farther."

I was glad that we didn't have to call her brother to tell him that we had lost her. We got back to the trailer, and I told May that she could shower first and change her clothes.

Paul was grabbing his stuff to head down to the campground showers. I stayed inside the trailer in case May needed anything. When she was finished, it was my turn. It felt so good to shower. I was glad to get the chlorine off me, and the dirt from the path that had stuck to my feet, let alone the perspiration from the worry of not finding them right off the bat.

When we had all had our showers, we tried to think of what to do next. Normally, Paul and I would read our books, but we knew that May was not a reader because her memory problem wouldn't allow her to like she once did.

We thought about playing cards, but that would be too hard for her as well, and we knew she wouldn't be able to play a board game either, so we went back outside to our lounge chairs and sat. I stretched mine out as far as it would go to lay back. After we were all settled in our chairs, May started to tell us the reason she had left the campsite, even though I had told her to stay there.

She said that Barkley was barking because he could see us over at the pool area. She said, "I thought if I could take him far enough away, to where he couldn't see you, that he wouldn't bark anymore."

The problem was, she got so turned around and couldn't remember her way back and had to go to the bathroom so badly, that she just sat down. I tried to make her feel better by telling her she did the right thing.

"I'm sorry that Barkley was being such a little shit," I said.

As I lay there on the lounge, I contemplated whether I had made a bad decision inviting May to come with us. Already our trip was not what I had thought it was going to be. I wasn't going to let her out of my sight. I think she dosed off because her eyes were closed, and she wasn't talking anymore.

Paul was reading his book and drinking a beer, and I was on the verge of falling asleep myself. My eyes were heavy, and the heat was getting to me, even though we had moved our chairs to the shade.

I decided to go inside the trailer and leave May asleep since Paul was next to her reading. I laid down on our bed to take a nap. The air conditioner had been running, and the trailer was almost cold. I really didn't mean to sleep as long as I did, but I woke up when Paul came in to use the bathroom.

I frantically asked, "Where's May?"

"She's ok, she's sitting in her chair," said Paul.

I hurried outside where she was alone. "Did you have a nice rest?"

"I didn't sleep."

I knew she had. I wondered why she wouldn't admit to dozing off.

It was time to start dinner, and we always barbecued when we went camping. Paul cooked the best steaks. I had made a potato salad, and it was ready to go. All I had to do was boil the corn on the cob.

This time May surprised me by asking, "Can I husk the corn for you?"

"That would be great, May."

I think she was glad to have something to do. When it was ready, we carried everything outside to eat on the picnic table. The sun had gone behind the clouds, and it felt nice outside.

The aroma of campers' grills floated through the air. If people hadn't started their dinners by now, the smells would get their juices flowing.

May raved about her steak saying, "This is the best steak I've ever had!"

It was a T-bone, and she was picking the little bits of meat that were stuck to the bone with her fingers, then licking them. It was a nice dinner.

Paul and I started to clean up, so May grabbed the butter and the sourdough bread and followed me into the trailer. I ran some soapy water in the small sink to do the dishes, while Paul cleaned the grill, and May continued to clean off the table. She put things on the counter since she didn't know where they went.

I thanked her for helping us. She offered to dry the dishes. I told her that we let them air dry in the drainer, and I would put them away before we went to bed.

I told her that I was going to change into long pants and a sweatshirt since it was cooling down as the evening was coming on. She did the same. When it was nightfall, the people who were camped next to us, the ones that we had asked if they had seen May, asked us if we wanted to join them to roast marshmallows and make s'mores over their fire pit.

I looked at Paul and May; they waited for me to answer.

"Sure, that would be fun."

Paul grabbed our folding chairs and took them over around their fire pit. They were from California and that started May talking about her relatives who lived there. They seemed genuinely interested in what she had to say. I think it made her enjoy herself even more.

She told them that she goes to California to visit her cousins every couple of years, but that she talks to them on the telephone every week. The way May was talking and laughing at things they said, you wouldn't have even known that she had Alzheimer's. At that exact time, she seemed so coherent.

It was fun to see her like that. We each had a s'more, and I made us all decaf coffees. We sat out until eleven o'clock, and by then, it had cooled down enough that we got cold and were shivering. We thanked the neighbors from California for a nice evening and walked a short distance back to our trailer.

Paul, Mayumi, and I took turns brushing our teeth and getting our pajamas on. I took Barkley out for his last time to go potty for the night, while Paul disassembled the table to make it into a bed for May.

We put plenty of warm blankets on in case she got cold during the night. We, on the other hand, slept with our bedroom window slightly open, but with plenty of blankets on us as well. I told Mayumi not to worry if she heard us get up in the night, having to go to the bathroom. We left a night light on for her, so it wasn't pitch black like it was outside. We went to sleep with Barkley snuggled between Paul and me.

I woke up to a noise I couldn't place. I listened and nudged Paul. "It sounds like someone is trying to get in our trailer."

He sat up and quickly grabbed his robe and a flashlight, and I followed him.

It was May, trying to unlock the door that went outside. I said, "May, what are you doing?

"I need to go to the bathroom."

"That door goes outside," said Paul. "The bathroom is right there, where the night light is, remember?"

"Oh," she said and went into the bathroom and shut the door.

I waited to make sure she made it back to bed, which she did.

Paul and I tried to go back to sleep, but neither one of us could get into a deep sleep after that, wondering whether she was going to try to go outside again.

Morning light couldn't come too soon.

When the light shone through our bedroom window, it seemed like we had just fallen asleep. I looked over at Paul snuggled under the covers with his eyes wide open.

He harshly said, "Never again."

I knew what he meant.

"Okay," I said humbly.

CHAPTER FIFTEEN

....

*T*HE CARE that a person with Alzheimer's requires, even in the early stages, is a lot. The person thinks they're fine to live on their own, not realizing what they can't remember.

What we had witnessed with May on this camping trip was worrisome. I was so looking forward to her joining in the fun times we had camping; but because of her memory problems, it turned out so different.

We didn't end up staying the full-time that we paid for. We felt it best to get her back home where she was used to being, where things were familiar. May didn't even realize that we cut the trip short because of her.

It takes such patience to be around a person who has Alzheimer's. We cared so much for May, and even our patience was put to the test. We packed up and headed home. Paul turned the radio up loud as we traveled because he didn't want to have to listen to the same stories that May always repeated, and we drove home without much conversation.

Days later after we were home from our fiasco of a camping trip, I decided to do some more research on Alzheimer's. I went to a website, Comprehending Alzheimer's.

It said that patients lead normal and productive lives in the initial phases of the disease. Stage One symptoms are mild. They face no difficulty communicating with other individuals. They can recall their way home, remember names, and can continue carrying out life's activities.

Stage Two is a slow decline in an individual's cognitive abilities. Individuals will experience memory loss, forget the names of loved ones, and also have trouble speaking to others. They suffer from decision-making problems. It said the patient's sleep cycle also gradually declines causing fatigue and laziness. Some patients even sleepwalk. Is that what we experienced with May? I wondered.

It went on to say that in the third or fourth stages, patients start to confuse the past with the present. Some patients eventually are confined to their beds and are at the mercy of their caregivers and eventually lose their ability to use their speaking or language skills because of the disease. I shut the computer off.

I was sick to my stomach. I was afraid of what the future held for my good friend.

I couldn't help but think that as you get to be a senior, the things that you need to remember are almost overwhelming. Passwords for every account you have, birthdays, using different remotes for every device, remembering appointments, how to use your iPhone, how to use your iPad and computer that seem to always be updating.

Passwords, passwords, passwords! Our friends say that their kids or grandkids have to help them with these things now that they are older, and we don't even have dementia or Alzheimer's, thank God. We have all read how important it is to keep our minds active. We have friends that read a lot, we have friends that put puzzles together and others who do word searches and crossword puzzles. Nobody wants memory problems like May struggles with, losing a little of her life bit by bit. That life-altering monster that can slowly creep up on you and strips you of your identity and who you are.

I told my friend about how AARP has a program called Staying Sharp. It has a brain health assessment that would be good to take, and games to make you use your brain and things to help you stay sharp. I was going to join. I was going to do what I could to have a clear mind. There were no guarantees.

It made me think about my mortality and the diseases from which my parents had died. Paul got after me for talking about it so much lately, and said, "Marcelina, let's enjoy the rest of the life that we have, and not worry about what's going to take us in the end. We can't change what's going on with May. All we can do is what we are doing for her. Letting her know we are here for her and helping her as much as we can."

I made a vow to myself; that's what I would do.

CHAPTER SIXTEEN

．．．．．．．．．．．．．．．．．．．．．．

*I*T WAS THE MONTH of November when my grand-daughter Gabriella called.

"Hi, sweetheart, how you are doing?"

"Fine Grandma, today in school we were learning about Día de los Muertos, Day of the Dead, and I told my teacher that I'm part Mexican."

An eighth to be exact, I snickered.

"My teacher asked me if my family celebrated Day of the Dead, and I told her no. I asked my mom if we could celebrate it, and she told me to call Grandma Marcelina, so that's what I'm doing," she said, in a cheerful voice. "Can we celebrate it, Grandma?"

"Sure, that'll be nice, honey."

Never having celebrated it before, the only thing I had to go by was the movie *Coco* by Disney. I thought about how I went to see that movie with my whole family and how much it touched my heart and made me cry, thinking of my older family members that had passed on. My mother, my dad, my brother, and my sister.

There was always a special place in my heart for my aunt Lucy who treated me with such kindness when I was young. Yes, I would do this with my granddaughter.

I picked up the DVD of *Coco* and studied the cover, looking for ideas to display on the table. I decided to go to the store to look for memorabilia for the Day of the Dead. I was so surprised that there was a full aisle devoted to this Mexican holiday. As I studied the items up and down the aisle, I carefully selected items that I thought would be pleasing to my granddaughter, but I didn't want to spend a lot of money.

As planned, Gabriella's mother dropped her off at one o'clock in the afternoon. I hugged her and thanked her for wanting to celebrate Día de los Muertos.

I had gathered pictures of those who had passed that I wanted to pay tribute to. I set up a table in the back bedroom and placed a tablecloth of multicolored flowers on top. I showed her the skull cookie cutters I had purchased and told her we were going to make them as an offering. She was so excited. I think that was her favorite thing I had bought, she loved to bake with me.

Gabriella and I started placing the pictures sporadically, and as we did this, I explained who each picture was, and why they were so special to me. She had never met any of these family members, but I could tell by the look on her face that she was absorbing the words and the love that I was conveying to her. And in return, I felt a special connection was made that day, between me and my granddaughter that would never be forgotten, because she wanted to embrace her Mexican heritage.

Gabriella was a beautiful girl. She had dark hair, olive skin, and amazing hazel eyes. People said she had an old soul and was very mature for her age. Her sister Sophie, though, was as light as Gabriella was dark.

Sophie had blonde hair, light skin, and beautiful blue eyes. She always looked out for Gabriella when they were very young, and they were always close. They reminded me of the sisters in the movie *Frozen*.

We placed a vase of colorful flowers on the table and a sign that said, Día de los Muertos. Skulls painted with bright colored paints were set in place. The cookies that Gabriella and I made were sugar cookies shaped like skulls, which was a big part of that holiday. We stood back and looked at our display, pleased with what we saw.

I said, "Let's call May and have her come over. I think she'll like this." Gabriella agreed. I never knew which phone to call her on. Some days she couldn't operate her cell phone, so I decided to call her on her landline which she still had, even though she couldn't remember how to retrieve her messages on it.

She answered after three rings, "Hello?"

"Hi, it's Marcelina, what are you doing?"

"I'm watching golf on TV," she said.

"I want you to come over to see something."

She didn't hesitate at all, happy for an invite of any kind. I didn't explain what it was about, but nonetheless, she ran over to my house across the lawn in her stocking feet. I already had our front door open to let the day's sunshine in. She timidly tapped on the glass of the storm door in her usual manner. I opened the door with Barkley barking at my feet.

"Hi, bud," she said and leaned down to pet him. "We didn't get our walk today, did we?"

He was happy to see her and rolled over to allow her to pet his belly.

My eleven-year-old granddaughter walked out of the back bedroom, and then May knew why we didn't go for our walk.

May looked up and said hi to Gabriella. She couldn't remember her name, though she has met Gabriella several times before, and had listened to Gabby, as we called her, talk about playing basketball on a county rec team.

Anything to do with sports sparked May's interest.

I didn't reintroduce them, but instead, asked Gabby to show May what we had been up to. May followed her to the back bedroom where we had our display. We still had our aprons on, covered in flour and dough as Gabriella grinned, showing her teeth lined with shiny braces. She was so proud of what we had created.

She offered May one of the skull cookies and explained how we had decided not to frost them because it would cover up the indentation of the face of the skull. "So, we left them plain," she said, "but they still taste good."

May agreed and took a second bite. She stared at the vibrant display. We explained to her what it was all about, and how Gabriella had encouraged me to do this. She apparently understood what we were saying and seemed to revel in the idea. She surprised us both when she asked if she could add a picture to our table. I had planned that the display was to be for our family only, so I was taken aback by her wanting to do that.

I said, "Yes," hoping she would forget about it after she got home.

Gabriella and I stood back and took pictures with our cell phones so that she could share them with her teacher at school. I asked Gabby and May if I could have a few minutes to offer a silent prayer to show my love and respect. They both bowed their heads in reverence, as I closed my eyes.

We went out of the room, and I left the battery-operated candles on. I didn't want to leave real candles burning for the three days that we were going to leave the display up to honor their lives, rather than mourn their death.

Every day I would go into that room and look at the display studying the pictures and remembering the part that each person played in my life. It felt good to take the time to remember.

On November 3rd, I started packing up the pictures and vowing to myself that I would continue with my photo albums and organize my family pictures that were stuffed in manila envelopes in a box. I gathered all the colorful decorations, as well as the tablecloth, and put them in a box labeled "Day of the Dead."

I didn't know if this would be an ongoing tradition with my granddaughter, but even if it wasn't, this had been a fulfilling, almost sacred experience for me.

CHAPTER SEVENTEEN

....

WEEKS LATER, I ran some spaghetti with meatballs over to May. It was a chilly November night, and she invited me in. All across her family room floor were pictures out of the box that had been sitting there for ages.

She said, "I finally found the picture that I want to add to your Day of the Dead celebration." In her mind, only a couple of days had gone by.

"It's too late, May. It's over. I packed it all up and put it away."

I knew that she felt bad that I hadn't reminded her, but I really just wanted my family's pictures there. I tried to change the subject when I asked her if she had eaten yet, and I handed her the bowl of spaghetti. She looked at me uncertainly, like she couldn't remember if she had eaten. Apparently, she had dumped the box of pictures out that morning and had been going through them all day.

Sadly, she said, "I wanted you to put this picture on your display."

She picked it up and handed it to me. It was a picture of a young man dressed in an Army uniform. A very handsome young man. I turned the picture over to see if there was a name on the back of it, but there wasn't. She stirred the pictures around on the floor until she found the other one that she wanted to show me. It was a picture of a Japanese American baby. She was staring at it with tears in her eyes.

I asked her, "Whose baby is this?"

She looked down and hesitated, then slowly answered, "Mine."

"Yours? I don't understand."

I knew there were times when I couldn't believe what she said, and there were times when she really couldn't remember and would get mixed up. I looked at the picture of the baby and noticed that he had the same dimples as the blond man in the picture. I'm sure I looked shocked. May had that same look on her face I had seen before when she is struggling hard to remember.

May seemed to have sudden clarity; it was like she was back in time, reliving the entire experience.

"My parents were against me dating Anthony." She pointed to the picture. "They wanted me to date a Japanese man who I bowled with for years. Akiro was his name, but Anthony and I continued to see each other without their permission. Going to places where we wouldn't see anybody we recognized.

"My brother Yuto was the only one who knew about us. My parents were old-fashioned. They didn't think that mixed races were a good idea."

I couldn't believe what I was hearing, or how she opened up to me. I think she knew by now, that I was not a person to judge or condemn. I softly urged her to go on, while her memory cooperated. I said, "Let's sit down."

I quickly pulled my cell out to text Paul, to tell him to go ahead and eat dinner without me, I was going to be awhile.

"Is everything okay?" he texted.

I answered, "Yes."

Mayumi said, "The blond man was a friend of my brothers who he had met while going to the university. They started doing things together, mostly golfing. They invited me to go along a couple of times, and the three of us had fun. He was really easy to be around, and I liked him."

She hesitated, and the look on her face seemed so far away. She squinted her eyes as she tried to dig deeper into her memory.

May continued.

"I didn't see him for months, and then one night,

my Japanese bowling team bowled against his team. We were so surprised to run into each other. He saw me first and walked over while I was polishing my bowling ball.

"'Is that you, Mayumi?'

"I looked up, and there stood beautiful Anthony. I said, 'yes, how are you? I didn't know that you bowled.'

"'There's a lot you don't know about me,' he said, in a flirty kind of way.

"It was time for my team to bowl against his team. I was self-conscious and felt a little nervous. I said to myself, I'm a good bowler and it doesn't matter who's watching me. Our team needs to win. I couldn't help but glance his way. He was so handsome and so Caucasian. I knew I had a crush on him. As the evening went on, I was able to relax. Our team was ahead. They were all having fun and drinking beer, while our team was competitive and set on winning, which we did. When the game was over, Anthony's team congratulated us and headed over to the corner of the bowling alley where there was a small bar, and they could continue drinking.

"Anthony slowly walked behind his buddies and told them he would be right there. He made his way over to me and asked if he could carry my bag out to the car. I was embarrassed because I could carry my bag, but I said, sure. As we walked out, I asked him if he was still golfing with Yuto.

"'Sometimes but not very often, I'm pretty busy.'

"We got to my car, and I opened the trunk, and he set the bag down. I thanked him, then he asked me, 'Do you think we could go out for a beer sometime?' I told him that I didn't drink, but we could go out for coffee or something else, so he asked me for dinner instead.

"I smiled, and said, okay. It was dark outside, and my heart was beating fast from the excitement of the night. All the way home I thought, why would he want to go out with me? I didn't tell my brother I ran into Anthony at the bowling alley. After all, he was drinking and might not even call me. Did I even want him to call me back? I must have because I kept waiting for our phone to ring after I arrived home from work the next day.

"Five days went by, and he hadn't called. I was a little disappointed but thought maybe it was better that he hadn't. The next week, I went to the bowling alley and met up with my team. I looked at various groups who were getting ready to compete. I didn't see him. In fact, I didn't see anyone from his team. I felt a little down when I finally realized that I wasn't going to see him tonight. Maybe that would be good for my game? I sat down and put my bowling shoes on and tried to psych myself up to be part of this team that was on a winning streak. I played with a vengeance, hitting the bowling pins with a sort of anger within me. Anger because I thought he liked me. Or anger because he didn't call me? Or probably anger from feeling stupid for believing him. I bowled my best game yet.

"'Let's keep this winning streak going,' our team captain said. Everyone patted me on the back and told me what a fantastic game I had. I was all smiles now, proud that I had such a high-scoring game. As I was putting my ball in the bag, I glanced over at the bar, and there drinking beer was Anthony with my brother Yuto. They both stood up and walked toward me.

"'Hey, that was one helluva game,' Anthony said to me, and my brother agreed with him.

"I asked them if they watched. They said they saw the second half.

"Anthony said, 'You were on fire. For being a little bit of nothing, you've got a mean swing with that ball.'

"I thought about the anger that I had felt and could feel my cheeks reddening. I wondered if he had told Yuto that he had asked if he could call me sometime. I hoped not. I didn't know how my brother would feel about me dating Anthony, let alone how my parents would feel. It made me feel good that he wanted to ask me out, and I made the decision to accept his offer to go, and not say anything to anyone else about it. We decided to meet at the restaurant so that he wouldn't have to come to my house. When I entered the restaurant, Anthony was already there. He smiled showing those dimples that I liked so much. He walked over to greet me. He was so handsome that it gave me butterflies in my stomach. He reminded me of Robert Redford, the actor, with that honey-colored hair and his perfectly shaped sideburns. What did he see in me, a simple Japanese girl? Maybe he was just trying to be polite because he was friends with my brother. I tried not to think about that and enjoy our evening together. We talked and laughed for hours. I couldn't believe how much we had in common, even though we were so different from one another. After that, we started seeing each other on a regular basis and eventually fell in love. I knew our parents wouldn't condone that. We had to sneak around, sometimes going to his apartment when we could. He called me his 'beautiful Japanese doll,' and I loved looking into his bright blue eyes. He was the only person that ever made me feel beautiful and loved.

"We dated for about a year. Neither one of us saw ethnicity or color. What we did see were equality and love. If only our parents could see that, but it was the sixties, and race mattered to so many people back then. Unrest was going on all over the country with every race, not just with black people. Interracial marriages were frowned upon."

In Mayumi's mind, she could remember his light skin against her brown skin, their lips softly touching. They were both virgins in a forbidden love affair.

"My parents urged me to continue seeing Akiro, a friend that bowled on my Japanese bowling team. Only because he was the same race as me. They even invited him over to dinner one night, when I had made plans to meet Anthony after I got off work. My mom had dinner ready, and he was visiting with them in the front room when I got home. I tried not to look disappointed when I saw him because, after all, he was a good friend. I liked him, but I didn't want to give him the impression that it was anything more, even though my parents would have wanted it to be.

"We sat down to dinner, and the whole time my thoughts were of Anthony, and what he would think since I hadn't shown up to meet him as we had planned. I couldn't call him on our home phone, for fear that my dad would hear me, and I couldn't risk that. The evening seemed to go by so slowly. Akiro was telling my parents all about his family back home in Hawaii. His father was a dentist, and his mother was a nurse. He went on to tell them what he was studying in college, and he was aware of how important an education was to his parents. They sounded like an ideal family. This conversation was only going to encourage my parents to insist that I date Akiro, but my heart would never let me abandon my dear Anthony. Akiro spoke Japanese, but his English was superb. I respected him, but I did not love him as my parents would have preferred me to do. I loved Anthony and knew I always would. When the evening grew late and I became quiet, Akiro could tell something was wrong.

"He got up and bid my parents farewell and said he needed to go home and study. I walked him to the door and stepped out onto the porch where my parents wouldn't hear me. I explained to him that I thought he was a very nice friend and I cared for him, but I was seeing someone else. He looked forlorn and asked me, 'Is it the guy I saw you with at the bowling alley the other night?' I said yes, not sure if he would be upset because he was Caucasian. If he was, he didn't say so. Instead, he hugged me and said that he would see me again sometime and wished me luck. I went back into the house, thankfully, my mom and Dad had gone to bed.

"Yuto my brother had come home through the back door and told me he had been with Anthony, and that he could tell that he was upset about something but wouldn't say what it was.

"I explained that I was supposed to meet Anthony, but the evening didn't go as planned. We talked in a hushed voice so our parents wouldn't hear us.

"Yuto hugged me and said, 'It's my fault, I should have never introduced you to Anthony.'

"Don't say that! We love each other. It's too late.

"He reminded me that Mom and Dad will never accept us being together.

"I said, well then, we'll run away. But Yuto pleaded with me not to do that. I told him I have to. I'm pregnant.

"Yuto's eyes got really big, and he asked me if Anthony knew.

"I told him, not yet. I was going to tell him tonight, but as you could see our parents had other plans for me. I couldn't get away. I asked him what did Anthony have to say tonight?

"Yuto said, 'He was grumpy and said that school wasn't going as well as he wanted it to and was thinking of dropping out. I tried to encourage him not to, and then after one beer he got up and left. He probably didn't want me to know that he was supposed to meet up with you.'

"I said goodnight to Yuto and kissed him on the cheek. I told him that he's a good brother, and

I thanked him for listening. Then I went into the kitchen to use the phone since Mom and Dad were asleep.

"I called Anthony's phone number and after three rings he picked up.

"I explained to him why I hadn't been able to meet him and talked about my frustration with my parents. I tried to talk as quietly as I could. I told him, we need to meet. I have something that I want to talk to you about.

"He said, 'When can you get away?'

"Friday after work. I overheard my mom remind my dad that they were going to a friend on Friday night to play cards.

"Anthony said, 'I hate to wait until Friday to see you. I love you so much.'

"I told him, I know, I love you too. See you Friday then, goodnight."

CHAPTER EIGHTEEN

AY TOLD ME more of the story with remarkable clarity.

"I went upstairs to bed and put my hands on my belly and thought of what was growing inside me. What was the baby going to look like? I hoped that it would look like Anthony. Would it be possible? Those bright blue eyes and deep-set dimples? I was happy but fearful of what my parents would say about a mixed-race baby. The thought made me shudder. I pulled the blankets up around my shoulders and fell asleep, thinking of Anthony.

"I was excited to be able to meet Anthony at the park. I drove straight to the spot where we had decided to meet. I sat in my car watching and waiting for his vehicle to drive up. The whole time I was contemplating how I was going to tell him that I'm pregnant and wondered how he would take it, and how he was going to tell his family. Anthony pulled up behind my car and got out. He put his arms around my small body and hugged me tight. I looked up at him, and he kissed my lips. My heart was pounding, knowing what I had to tell him.

"We walked around the park until we found a secluded picnic table. Anthony had picked up some chicken for our dinner. As we ate, we talked about our jobs and about Anthony wanting to quit college. I really was a little disappointed that he didn't want to continue his education. I couldn't help but think how important an education was to Akiro, and how much he appreciated the opportunity his parents provided for him to go.

"Then I asked my handsome lover, what do you want to do if you quit school?

"He said, 'I'm still young, I have plenty of time to decide what I'm going to do.'

"I felt like this was not the time to tell him about the baby, he was too unsettled. We decided to walk down by the pond, and we stood there, hand in hand looking at our reflections in the water. Caucasian and Japanese. We didn't see any difference. I laid my head on Anthony's shoulder, and he kissed the top of my head.

"I wondered if I should tell him now while it's so peaceful out here? Just then, a couple came up behind us. It was an older couple that I recognized.

I pulled away from Anthony and dropped his hand. It was my mother's friends. I wondered why they weren't playing cards with my parents.

"I greeted them and introduced Anthony as my friend.

"This is Mr. and Mrs. Massimera, my parent's good friends.

"They looked Anthony up and down. I hoped they thought he was a nice-looking young man as I did. Could they tell we were in love? Or could we pull it off as just being friends?

"My parents' friends said they needed to get going because they were going to meet my parents to play cards. I looked at my watch, it was twenty minutes to seven, and I knew they played cards at seven o'clock. I told them that it was good to see them again, and they quickly headed toward the parking lot to leave.

"When they were gone, I said to Anthony I hope they don't mention seeing me with you tonight.

"My parents had met Anthony when he would do activities with Yuto, but they had no knowledge of me being with him for over a year. Running into my parent's friends completely changed my mood. I was tired of sneaking around and said so to Anthony.

"He said, 'So let's not anymore. Let's tell your parents that we are in love, and we want to get married.'

"That was the first time that marriage had come

up, and Anthony suggested we go to his apartment and talk, where we can be alone. We left my car there and rode together.

"'Get that skinny ass over here,' he teased.

"I slid over as close to him as I could, without sitting on his lap. He put his hand on my knee and held the steering wheel with the other one.

"I loved being so close to him and smelling his Elsha cologne. He always smelled so good. Once inside Anthony's apartment, we were both disappointed to see that his roommate was there.

"He had a popular sixties band blaring. We hoped the roommate would sense that we wanted to be alone and leave, but it was apparent that he was studying and had no plans of going anywhere.

"I felt uncomfortable sitting on Anthony's bed where we made love for the first time.

"The guys ruffled each other's hair and punched each other in the arm. Anthony ignored me, and I felt like an outcast.

"After they were done teasing each other, Anthony said, 'Let's get out of here and let this geek study.'

"He flipped the peace sign to his roommate and said, peace brother. We left, not having discussed anything.

"I was disappointed and upset. Anthony drove me back to where we left my car. He hoped we could make out before we parted for the night, but I was not in the mood. I was concerned about our future together.

"I told him I need to get home. I have to work tomorrow and I'm tired.

"So, Anthony kissed me goodbye and left frustrated. I knew my parents would still be playing cards, and I was glad.

"I went in to take a shower where I could cry, and nobody would hear me or ask why I was crying.

"After I got into my pajamas, I heard the phone ring downstairs. I knew it was Anthony because I had told him my parents were out for the evening.

"When I answered, he said right away that he was sorry about tonight. I told him I was sorry too. He said you mean so much to me, Mayumi. I don't care what anybody thinks, we are going to be together. It felt good to hear him say those words. He said his parents were coming into town next week to visit, and he wanted me to meet them.

"I asked if he was sure, and he said yes, they will love you if I love you. You'll see.

"I was nervous thinking about meeting Anthony's parents. Would they feel like my parents felt, that he should stay with his own kind? He said they were good people, maybe they would just want happiness for their son, I hoped. I wondered if Anthony had mentioned me at all to his parents, or would it be a complete surprise dropped on them? I wanted to bring that up with Anthony before I met them.

"All week I tried to think of the perfect time to tell Anthony of my little secret growing inside me, but I wanted to wait to see if his parents accepted me or not. I made an appointment at a beauty salon to have my long black hair trimmed before meeting Anthony's parents. I was nervous.

"That night at dinner, my parents continued to talk about Akiro and what a good catch he would be. They talked about what a nice Japanese family he had. Then my mom said a relative of hers was getting married to a nice Japanese fellow, and they were going on a honeymoon in Japan.

"I had almost had enough and wanted to yell We are Americans Mama not just Japanese! I felt the pressure building within me. I looked over at my brother Yuto and thought, why don't you say something? Why don't they pressure you? They don't seem to care who he dates. He's free to do as he pleases, yet he never brings his dates home.

"I knew that he dated girls that were not Japanese. I had seen them at the bowling alley bar, where he liked to hang out. Obviously, I knew I would disappoint my parents with the choice I made and needed to make it known fast.

"To my relief, Yuto finally seemed to get the drift and changed the subject.

"He said, 'Pop, did you hear that the Red Sox won their game?'

"That was all it took for my dad and brother to talk about sports the rest of the night. I was so thankful to Yuto. I helped Mom clean up the dishes and told her how good the Japanese food was that she had made.

"Mom said that she needed to teach me to make Japanese food for my husband one day. I agreed that would be nice.

"I dropped the glass plate I was drying, and it shattered to the floor.

"I said sorry, and with shaky hands, I started to pick up the bigger pieces.

"Mom noticed and asked, what is the matter 'Anaya,' which means dear in Japanese.

"I started to cry, and Mom put her arms around me and suggested we sit down.

"It all came pouring out. I told Mom that I had been seeing Anthony for over a year, and how much he meant to me. That we were in love. I could see the disappointment on Mother's face, and she started to speak in Japanese, saying that your father was not going to like this, he had other plans for you.

"I pleaded with her. Please, Mama, talk to Daddy,

it's not his choice, it's my choice who I love.

"But she shook her head, not agreeing with me.

"Listen to me, Mama there's more – I'm pregnant and Anthony doesn't know it yet.

"My mother looked aghast. 'Pregnant?' she repeated.

"I replied, yes, just barely. As if that made things any better, I thought.

"It felt so good to tell someone, even if I knew my mom was disappointed in me and knew my father would be too. Mom agreed to talk to my dad when the time was right. In the meantime, I needed to decide when the time would be right to tell Anthony now that my parents would know.

"My dad was a stern man, and his old Japanese values were important to him. Would I disgrace our family? I hugged my mom and told her I was going up to bed. The emotion of it all had taken its toll on me. I passed my dad sitting in his easy chair smoking a cigarette and watching a ball game. He didn't look up, and I was glad since my eyes were red from crying. I took off my shoes so that he wouldn't hear me going up the stairs. Once inside the confines of my bedroom, I sat by the window and looked out at the stars, wondering if Anthony's parents had come into town yet, and if he had prepared them to meet me. Would he tell them beforehand that I was Japanese?

The week went on, and my mother never brought the subject up again.

"I was to meet Anthony's parents on Saturday night. We would all go to dinner at a popular steakhouse. I made sure Anthony didn't pick me up at my house until my mom had time to talk to my dad, which hadn't happened yet.

"I met him at his apartment. His roommate was gone this time, and it made it nice for us to converse before I was to meet his parents. I still kept to my plan of not telling him about the baby until after meeting his parents.

"He asked, 'Should we tell my parents that we want to get married?'

"You haven't even asked me yet, silly.

"He said you know I love you. I replied I know. Let's just see how the evening goes.

"Anthony started kissing my neck until his lips eventually found my lips and then he kissed me with urgency. I loved kissing him but knew we had time restraints and said, we better go before we get into something we can't stop.

"Anthony said, 'We have time,' and started kissing me more aggressively.

"No, Anthony, we need to talk about what we are going to say tonight. Let's not mention anything about marriage yet, okay?

"'Okay,' he sounded frustrated, but said, 'My parents are going to love you. They'll see how sweet you are, and how happy you make me. What they won't be happy about is me quitting college.'

"He stepped away from me and looked around knowing that the time was near. He said, 'I don't want to study. I just want to be with you.'

"The next morning at breakfast Yuto didn't say anything about last night to our parents. That would only justify their feeling of staying with their own race. Yuto was good at keeping my secrets to himself. We were close, and he always watched out for me. He knew how much I appreciated it. I knew he would be there for me no matter what. He knew our parents were old-fashioned, trying to hang on to their heritage and be American at the same time. It wasn't easy for us kids, and it was even harder for our parents. Discrimination was unrelenting, and it was everywhere. Anyone who looked different had a hard time. I could understand my parents' point of view wanting me to marry someone Japanese. It would make things simpler, but you can't help who you love.

"My mom finally found the right time to tell my dad about my fretful situation. He was so upset that he banged his fist on the coffee table and made the teacups rattle. I was in the kitchen at the time, and

I knew by the loud sound that she had told him. I dreaded coming out of the kitchen to bring them sweet bread to have with their tea, but I knew I had to face the consequences.

"My dad was not a mean man, but he believed that what he said was law. After all, he was the head patriarch of our family, and he didn't like his authority questioned. I came into the front room feeling the flush of my face. His dark brown eyes looked frightening to me. I set their cakes on the coffee table.

"My dad said, in a very stern voice, 'Sit down, Mayumi. Your mother tells me that Yuto's blonde friend has gotten you in trouble?'

"It's not like that, Daddy, we love each other. I want to be with him. I was crying. I knew Dad couldn't believe what he was hearing. He yelled, 'NO, YOU MUST NOT! Has he said that he would take care of you and this baby?'

"I hesitated and said, well, he doesn't know about the baby yet, but I know he wants to be with me.

"Dad started yelling in Japanese this time, telling me to never see him again, and that I was an ungrateful daughter, that I would give the family a bad name.

"I was sobbing now and felt ashamed. Dad told Mom that they were going to have to send me away before anyone found out.

"I said, you can't do that to me. I love him!

"Dad wouldn't listen to any explanations or reasoning. He demanded that arrangements be made immediately for me to go stay with an aunt until the baby was born, and then it would be put up for adoption. Mother nodded in dutiful agreement. I couldn't believe what I was hearing. I couldn't even look at my dad, he was too furious.

"I ran up the stairs and slammed my bedroom door. I cried all night, wondering what I was going to tell Anthony. The next morning, I got ready for work and couldn't wait to leave the house. I would use the phone at work to call Anthony and tell him what went on last night and that my parents were sending me away. My thoughts were not on my job as they should have been, I had more difficult things to think about. Besides the fact I was tired from not sleeping well because I was up all night sobbing.

"I stood up from my desk and went into the break room to get some coffee. I felt sick. I sat at a small table in the corner and thought of my situation. My heart was breaking. How could I leave Anthony, who had chosen me to love, when I knew he could have had any girl on campus? How was I so lucky he had chosen me? I tried not to cry in case one of my co-workers came into the break room, I didn't want to have to explain.

"They were probably hard at work, as I should be. After I had a few sips of coffee and some saltine crackers, I headed back to my desk, not saying good morning to anyone I knew. I could possibly be leaving in a few weeks anyway. I tried Anthony's phone one more time, and there was no answer. I decided I had better leave a message."

"Hi, it's me. Call me as soon as you can, and I hung up the phone.

"I didn't want to go into any detail in case his roommate got the messages first. The day went by slowly, and I spent a good amount of time in the bathroom throwing up. I never received a call back from Anthony. When it was five minutes to five, I clocked out and couldn't get out of there fast enough. I drove straight to Anthony's apartment. I knocked on the door, and no one answered. I knocked again and thought maybe they were playing music and couldn't hear.

"Still, no one answered the door. I decided that it was important enough that I would sit on his front steps and wait for him to come home. Just as I was about to go because I couldn't wait any longer to go to the bathroom, I saw Anthony walking toward me.

"His golden hair was slightly windblown, and he had the starting of a matching mustache coming in.

I liked it, and I felt butterflies in my stomach. Or was it the baby?

"When Anthony reached me, he said, 'Well, what a nice surprise!'

"He put his arms firmly around me and kissed me with passion. He didn't look around to see who could see us. He didn't hold back. He loved me.

"Feeling a little conspicuous, I said let's go inside.

"He looked at my serious expression and agreed to go in. Once inside, he asked me, 'What's wrong?'

"My parents have found out about us.

"He replied, 'Good. Now we don't have to sneak around anymore.'

"No, there's more. I hesitated. I'm pregnant, Anthony.

"'What? I thought we were being careful?'

"Obviously not as careful as we thought. My dad is furious with me and said terrible things and demanded that I not ever see you again.

"Anthony replied, 'They can't stop us, May, we'll get married.'

"I stopped him in his tracks. They're sending me away, Anthony, and I started to cry.

"'No baby, I won't let them.'

"He started kissing me up and down my neck.

"I pulled away and said, 'You don't know my dad very well, he may have been nice to you when you were with Yuto, but he's a determined man not to have the family's reputation be tarnished.'

"'We'll think of something,' he said, 'I'll get a full-time job and take care of you and our little one, you'll see.'

"I'd better get home, or they'll know that I've been with you. I kissed him goodbye and left."

Mayumi drove home and felt relief that she had finally told Anthony about the baby. It made her feel good when he said, "We'll think of something."

When she got home, dinner was ready, and they all sat down to eat, including Yuto. It was an un-usually quiet dinner. May kept her head down, not wanting to meet her father's eyes. She had felt sick all morning and now had a ferocious appetite. She hoped that she would be able to hold her dinner down. Nothing was said about her being sent away, but she was sure it wouldn't be forgotten.

She was to meet Anthony at their usual Friday night meeting place, then they would plan. When dinner was over, Mayumi helped her mother with the dishes as she normally did. While she had time alone with her mother, she begged her to talk with her dad to let her stay home, and not be sent away.

"Please, Mama."

Her mother looked at her sympathetically, "It is not my decision."

Mayumi cried as she dried the dishes.

"Mama, don't you remember when you were young and in love?"

"It was different, he was not white."

This stung May. Why were they so prejudiced when their whole family had experienced problems with people being prejudiced against them?

"We want what's best for you," her mother said.

Mayumi didn't see Anthony until Friday. When they were together, it seemed like everything would be okay. She told him how every day she had morning sickness at work and spent a good part of the mornings in the bathroom.

He said, "I'm sorry you're so sick. I wish there was something I could do."

He rubbed the hardly visible bump that was now forming within her stomach. May asked Anthony if he had told his parents yet. He hesitated. "Yes. They're not very happy with me, but let's not talk about that right now. Let's enjoy our time together."

She wore a loose-fitting gray floral blouse that looked good with her shiny black hair. "You look beautiful tonight, Mayumi."

They decided they would go to a drive-in movie together not caring what the movie was, as long as they could be together. Mayumi liked drive-in movies where you could roll your windows down and be in the comfort of your car; comfort these days meant a lot to her.

Once they got the speaker placed on the car window, they turned the volume up. They pushed their seats back as far as they would go, to allow them more space. It was a beautiful night, and May said it felt good to feel Anthony's arm around her.

Mayumi laid her head on Anthony's shoulder. The movie was a comedy, and they both welcomed the good endorphins that laughter brought them. They didn't really want to see what was playing next.

"I don't want to go yet," Anthony said, "I want to be with you every minute I can."

He leaned over and kissed her, and she sweetly kissed him back. They stayed later than they had intended, not watching the movie at all.

By the time Mayumi got home, it was very late, and her dad was waiting up for her. The minute she shut the front door to creep up the stairs, he stood in front of her. "You've been with him, haven't you?"

May didn't answer.

"I told you, you were to never see him again!" he yelled, in a thunderous voice. "You sneaked behind our backs; you degrade our family by expecting a baby out of wedlock. You need to learn obedience! Pack your clothes. You're going to live with your aunt in California in the morning."

Mayumi couldn't believe what she was hearing. They were sending her away immediately! She ran up the stairs crying out loud, not even offering a rebuttal for herself.

Her mother must have known what her dad was going to say because she didn't come downstairs.

May cried herself to sleep, and very early in the morning, her mother woke her and told her to bring her bag and come downstairs.

Her eyes were red and swollen from crying all night. Mayumi felt a panicky feeling come over her. She needed to get hold of Anthony and tell him what was going on. She would send a message to him through Yuto.

That's it, Yuto would do that for her. She ran back upstairs to his room, not bothering to knock. She just burst in and shook him out of a deep sleep.

"You must tell Anthony that Mom and Dad are sending me away, they're sending me to San Francisco with Auntie Suzi! You've got to help me, brother!"

He looked at her frantic face, as tears were coming down.

"Tell him I will call him when I can. Yuto, tell him that I love him. Let him know how Daddy is, that there is nothing I can do right now."

Just then her dad yelled upstairs in his strong authoritative voice, telling her that she needed to come down, they were going now.

Mayumi kissed Yuto goodbye. He followed May downstairs and tried to change their father's mind, but it only made him angrier saying, "it's none of your business!"

He told him to shut his mouth, in Japanese. It was no use. He grabbed Mayumi and hugged her tight and promised he would get hold of Anthony.

CHAPTER NINETEEN

....

*L*IVING AT AUNTIE SUZI'S HOUSE was different from living with her parents. Auntie was kind and would listen to Mayumi's point of view. Auntie knew that things were different from when she was young, and even more changes were coming. She wanted Mayumi's life to be good. She felt bad that she was in this predicament. She was a kind woman, and Mayumi felt her auntie's love.

Mayumi was halfway through her pregnancy and talked with Anthony on the phone every week. He told her that he would come and take her away, but the longer she was there, the more she thought that it would be better to have the baby there. She liked the doctor that Auntie had found for her.

"Let's wait," she said to Anthony.

"Ok, my love, one day we will be together."

That's what kept Mayumi going. Her aunt took her to her doctor appointments, and they would go out for clam chowder afterward and make a day of it. Mayumi liked living in San Francisco. Everyone seemed so accepting there. The community that her aunt lived in was predominantly Japanese, but she had friends outside the confines who were Caucasian. She seemed really open-minded for being as old as she was, yet she would tell Mayumi about their ancestors who lived in Japan, how different their lives were from hers, and how lucky she felt to live the good life that she was living. But she reiterated, "We must never forget our ancestors. We are Japanese, and we must be proud of it."

Mayumi was glad to be away from her dad. Her mother called regularly to check on her pregnancy and to hear about how her doctor appointments went. She hoped her mother was softening a bit about her being pregnant.

Mayumi wrote letters to Anthony several times a week but lately hadn't received a letter back. Her brother Yuto called that night and told her Anthony was going to join the Army. He couldn't stand her being gone, and he couldn't find a full-time job like he wanted to.

He was frustrated and believed that if he joined the Army, he would be able to stash money away for the day that they would be a family.

Mayumi didn't know what to say to Yuto. She

knew that Anthony had quit school, despite his parent's objections, but why didn't he call her and let her know of his plans? Mayumi started crying and told Yuto to have Anthony call her when he could. She wanted to hear it from his lips.

Yuto said that he would and hung up.

Mayumi was seven months along now and had only heard from Anthony once, telling her that he had been in basic training and how rigorous it was.

He didn't say anything about the baby or ask her how she was feeling. She wondered if he was losing interest in her. It seemed like lately, all she did was cry. Two more months and she needed to decide what she was going to do about keeping the baby. Her aunt had talked to an adoption agency in San Francisco. She had promised Mayumi's parents that she would carry out the plan that was asked of her.

She had talked to Mayumi about it in the past, but she would only get hysterical, but now that Anthony seemed to be slipping away, she wondered if that might be the best thing to do. She could feel the baby moving around all the time now. She wondered how could she agree to forfeit her baby that was conceived in love. Was it a boy or a girl? Did Anthony still love her? All these questions weighed heavy on her.

She started to wonder if maybe her parents were right. She should have dated Akiro, he would not have gotten her into this predicament. He would have stayed in college, and they would not have people judging them for mixed races. She said life became so overwhelming, that it would have been better not to have to make all of these hard decisions.

She didn't know what to do. In Mayumi's ninth month of her pregnancy, she got word that Anthony was at war in Viet Nam. In her last letter to him, she explained that she needed to decide whether she would keep their baby or put it up for adoption. She didn't know if the letter had reached him or not, since he was no longer stationed at the address she had for him.

She told me that she knew in her heart that Anthony would not want her to put their baby up for adoption. She was sure he still loved her, and she still loved him.

May said her parents came to be with her the week the baby was due. They asked her right away if the adoption agency had found a family who was willing to adopt the baby.

She told them they were looking, but she still held out hope that she would receive a letter from Anthony.

Instead, she received a phone call from Yuto saying that Anthony's parents called him, and Anthony had been killed in Viet Nam.

May said Yuto was crying and told her he was sorry.

Mayumi said her whole body went limp, and she fell to the floor, devastated by the bad news. Her parents rushed over to her to help her up, but she wanted nothing to do with them in her grief.

Auntie came over, put her arms around Mayumi, and let her sob until she was worn out. Yuto said he was going to come to California to be with her, but she was too numb to care. Nothing could stop her world from coming down. She would never feel that kind of love again.

The sadness overwhelmed her in the days to come, and depression set in. She couldn't eat, she couldn't sleep. All she could do was cry.

Even Yuto was of no help to her. He told her that the Army was going to send Anthony's body to his hometown, and his parents would let him know when the funeral was going to be.

That made Mayumi cry even harder. She knew she would not be able to go. She felt so alone, even though her whole family was there now. A few days went by, and Mayumi started to feel pain again.

It was late at night, as she lay there in her bed. She said she had wondered if this was the real thing and if she should wake anyone. She said she lay there for over an hour until she couldn't stand the pain any longer, then went to wake her mother.

She softly shook her mother and said, "I think I'm in labor."

Her water hadn't broken yet, but she was having severe pains. They drove her to the hospital where she was admitted.

This was it.

She was going to have Anthony's baby, and Anthony was dead.

Mayumi's aunt made sure it was a Japanese doctor who was to deliver Mayumi's baby, as requested by her parents.

The delivery was hard and long. She was such a small girl that she was in a tremendous amount of pain. Sweat was running down her face and neck. Mayumi was not only in physical distress, she was in emotional distress. They had a hard time getting the baby out. When the last horrendous pain came, she screamed out Anthony's name and said, "I can't do this without you!"

She was exhausted. Black sweaty strands of hair stuck to her face. Her mother started to panic as Mayumi fell back into the pillow.

Her mother continued holding Mayumi's hand and said something to the doctor in Japanese.

He looked up at the monitors and could see that Mayumi's heart rate was slowing down.

"Please, Mayumi, work with me," he said, "one more hard push."

The nurse leaned Mayumi up, and her mother firmly held her back. She pushed with all the strength that she could muster, and the doctor was able to get the baby out safely.

Mayumi fell back as she heard the cry of a baby.

"It's a boy!" the doctor announced.

The nurse put the baby in Mayumi's arms. She was so weak, she could hardly hold him. She looked down at the fuzzy patch of black hair on his head and his small, wrinkled face. She could see that he looked like Anthony, those same dimples already apparent. Her beautiful Anthony. She started to sob.

Her mother leaned over and said, "Don't cry, it's all over now, the adoption agency has found a couple to adopt him."

HIM, she thought, who didn't even have a name, HIM, who didn't have a father.

She hesitated, and in her exhaustion exclaimed, "I want him to be named Anthony Jr," then she quickly asked them to take the baby to the nursery, she wanted to be alone in her grief.

Mayumi slept and slept. She had dreams of her and Anthony together, happy and in love. She was in and out of sleep confused as to what was real and what was not.

The nurse was at her side asking her to drink some juice and gave her a couple of pills to take. Then it all came flooding back to her. The baby. What was she going to do? She knew what her parents wanted her to do. The nurse asked if she was ready to have her baby brought back in, and she said no.

The nurse looked at her sadly but knew the situation. Mayumi's mother came back into the room, and Yuto was with her this time. She told them she would sign the adoption papers.

Yuto didn't look at her, he kept his head down as if he was studying the pattern of the tiles on the floor. She knew her mother would be happy, even if she wasn't.

Six weeks later Mayumi left her auntie's house and went back home to her parents. She never saw her little Japanese/American baby again.

I couldn't believe what May had just confessed to me, and how clearly she could remember it all. Never in all the years that we had been friends, had she even hinted at something like this.

She never found love like that again.

It was late, and I promised May that I would never speak of her story to anyone, not even Paul. She would probably never have such a long time of clarity to ever remember it again. I told her we would make a special scrapbook of all the people who were dear to her and display it on her coffee table. She never brought it up again. The last time I went into her house the pictures were cleaned up, and the box was out of sight. Possibly Yuto had stored those pictures in the basement with the other faded memories.

I thought about how much May had been through in her life, discrimination, not being able to marry who she wanted, or make her own decisions about her baby. If her situation had been nowadays, nobody would care who she was dating, or if couples were of the same race.

Mixed-race partners were seen all the time. Girls shouted out in front of Planned Parenthood, "My body, my decision." Having babies and not being married is more and more accepted by families. My friend made me see things differently. I was glad that things were changing. They might be baby steps, but I thought they must keep moving forward.

CHAPTER TWENTY

....

PAUL WAS GOING TO TAKE our grandson Oakley to the copper mine. My dad had worked there for over thirty years, and yet I hadn't ever been there before. I was pleased that Paul wanted to spend some one-on-one time with Oakley.

I decided since they would be gone all day, I would spend some time with May to get her out of the house. That's the thing that I liked about our friendship, she was always available at the drop of a hat, yet it was always at my convenience, when I felt like it, not her.

I didn't feel pressured or feel like I had to do it. I truly enjoyed her company. Paul was on his computer looking up information on the copper mine, when it was open if there were tours available, and how to get there.

He was always prepared and would search for information on things he was going to do. I didn't know if our grandson was especially excited to go to the mine, but he knew his outing with his grandfather always ended in his choice of where he wanted to go to lunch.

I called May on her landline, and she didn't answer. I tried to call her cell phone, and she didn't answer that either. It was always a concern when I couldn't reach her. I thought I'll try again in a little while, it's still early.

I sat back down on the couch to start reading the book I had started the day before yesterday, I was eager to get back to it. Paul was already engrossed in searching the internet when I interrupted him.

"I'm really glad you're taking Oakley up to where my dad worked, I think he'll be amazed."

"I hope so."

Then, it was as if a light went on, and he asked, "Did you want to go with us?"

"No, you two go, it's good for you to spend time with your grandson. It won't be long before he won't want to do that anymore. Being with friends will be the only thing he'll care about."

We had seen that with some of our older grandchildren.

Time was going so fast, and I began to recognize May's good days and her bad days.

On her good days, she would talk up a storm

about the past. On bad days which were more frequent now, she would walk slowly and look around as if she didn't recognize where we were going, even though we generally took the same path.

The trees on both sides of the trail were still barren of leaves, and it was muddy in spots from the melted snow. I decided to take her through a neighborhood that was adjacent to ours. The houses were nice tall brick homes with well-kept yards, even this early in the year.

May finally spoke up and started pointing out spring flowers that were in bloom. She started talking about her mother and how she had planted a lot of spring bulbs years back, and how she loved to work in her garden.

Of course, I had heard that many times over, but it felt good to hear her talk about her mother and how they did everything together. May was a good daughter.

As we walked further into the neighborhood, we both had to shed our sweatshirts and tied them around our waists. We were walking at a pretty good pace now and were talking as fast as we walked. We notice the warmer it got, the people were out in their front yards puttering around, seemingly glad like us to be outside.

Some would say good morning, and we would

respond in unison, "Good morning." I wondered, if exercise helped with Alzheimer's, or was it being around other people that helped her? It seemed like it, but I wasn't sure.

May had a family member put her contacts in her phone since she couldn't remember their phone numbers. Because she lived alone, her phone became her companion. She would call people and would talk for hours. When she would leave her house, she would never remember to take her cell phone with her. She didn't remember how to retrieve her messages, so it was useless to leave her one. Sometimes she would have a hard time and would tell us that she lost all her contacts. We would tell her to bring her phone over, and we would help her, and of course, her contacts were still there.

Paul and I would show her step-by-step how to get her messages, but we would have to show her all over again. Her memory problem would not let her remember what we had shown her. Sometimes she would call people in the middle of the night, not realizing what time it was. When family members would tell her it was four o'clock am, she would nervously say, "sorry," and quickly hang up.

She did that to Paul and me a couple of times.

Because May was beginning to forget what day and time it was, I sat down with her one day at my house and said, "I want to help you. I'm going to order you a clock. It has big numbers, the date, and the day of the week."

I always thought it was weird that she didn't have a single clock in her house. She depended on her cell phone for the time but couldn't keep track of it.

We searched on Amazon and found the perfect one. Below the time, it had the date, including the year. I was so excited to find it for her and thought how helpful it would be. She thought that sounded good.

When it was delivered, I called May and asked her to come over and see it. We opened it with anticipation, like kids opening a Christmas present. It was just what she needed, but I couldn't get it to light up.

I called Paul in. "Honey, can you take a look at this clock I ordered for May, please? It's not working."

He immediately discovered that it didn't have a battery in it, and of course, it was a specialty battery for clocks, which neither one of us had. We ran to Walgreens, and we were able to get the battery. The clock was perfect for her. I told her to take it home and put it somewhere in full view, where she could see it every day.

But it got so that even when she looked at it, the time didn't register with her anymore.

The clock was all lit up, but the light inside her head was dimming.

I remembered when May told me about one day when she went into her mom's bedroom and said she stared at the same faded bedspread from when her mom was alive. Her mom's clothes were still in the closet after all these years. It was obvious to me that she missed her mother so much.

She said she laid her head on the bedspread, and it smelled old and dusty. She said she could picture her mom's face clearly when she was sitting at her sewing machine. May told me it had felt so real.

It was hard for her to understand why she could remember all of that, but she couldn't remember appointments and other things.

She told me that she had grabbed her mom's robe and put it on. She said she cried out to her mother, but there was no answer. Then she whispered, please help me but no answer came. The robe felt like her mother's arms around her, and she wept.

I made a large taco casserole for Paul and me, so I decided to take some over to May.

I rang the doorbell. It took a few minutes for May to open the door, and when she did, she was cradling her left elbow.

I asked her what had happened. She invited me in and explained she had just woken up and felt confused. She said she couldn't tell what time of day it was; that she felt lightheaded and couldn't find her cell phone.

She said she had looked around in her bed and had moved clothes and boxes, but she couldn't remember where she had used it last.

She told me she made a cup of coffee hoping it would help her think more clearly. Her television was on, so she watched it to see when the weatherman told her what day it was.

May said she thought she had blacked out, she was scared, and she couldn't remember anything. She said she had gone into the bathroom to see if she had left her phone on the counter.

I had noticed before that her counter was crowded with lotions, mouthwash, and hand sanitizers among other things. She said when she reached to move things around on her counter to find her phone, she tripped on the rug and hit her elbow on the toilet.

She said she lay on the floor in pain, but finally

got up and pushed her shirt up to look at her elbow. She said the pain was radiating up her arm, and it was starting to swell.

It scared her to wake up in the afternoon thinking it was morning and on top of it couldn't find her phone. She said she had never felt this frightened in her entire life.

She said, "I can't keep things straight anymore."

I hugged her and told her that I missed her for our morning walks, that I hadn't seen her for a couple of days, and that I had been worried about her.

She had no explanation. Her face was blank. She had no idea how many days she had slept, or lost track of time, only that she was ravenous.

I told her to eat the dinner I had brought and that I would check on her tomorrow.

May seemed so vulnerable and said, "I am so lucky to have you and Paul as neighbors."

I think May knew we truly cared about her, and that we watched over her.

The next day, May told me that people were coming into her house and taking things. She said her purse and her cell phone were missing.

I asked her who she thought might be doing that. She said she didn't know, but she was going to call her brother to come over and help her.

When he came over, I just stood back and watched. Yuto asked her what she was missing.

She told him her cell phone, and that she thought it was in her purse, but she couldn't find it either.

Yuto looked in May's closet and found her purse amongst her shoes. He brought it to her, but her phone was not in it.

He looked under the adult coloring books and newspapers stacked on the ottoman, but it wasn't there. He pulled the blankets off the couch, and the remote control dropped onto the floor. Apparently, she had told him before that someone had taken that too.

Yuto told her no one was taking her things, and he was sure her phone would show up soon. He looked up at me, and I nodded.

May wasn't convinced.

Yuto tried to make her feel better telling her, "We all misplace things, May, we're all over sixty for hell's sake."

She didn't find that funny.

Her brother gave her a big hug and assured her that everything was going to be okay.

On the way home, the reality of May's situation hit Yuto hard. It was so depressing to him to watch the gradual decline of his once vibrant sister. He knew something had to be done and decided to call a family meeting to determine how to move forward in helping Mayumi.

CHAPTER TWENTY-ONE

....

I WALKED OUT onto the deck. Mayumi was sitting next to her tomatoes in her mother's robe.

I said, "Good morning, May, how are your tomatoes doing?"

She didn't seem to know where the sound was coming from.

She slowly answered, "They're doing okay."

"I'm going to make us some lunch in a little bit, and I'm going to make those good turkey sandwiches with cheese that you like so much. Would you like to come over?"

May tossed the robe onto her deck. She always had a hard time opening the gate that led to our backyard, and we usually kept it locked. Barkley heard her and started barking and wagging his tail. He always recognized his walking friend.

Paul walked over and helped unlatch the gate, and said, "Hi there."

May reached down to pet the dog. She said, "I've missed you, buddy."

He immediately jumped up on her pants, letting her rub his sandy-colored fur. Paul told her to sit under the gazebo.

Paul put his rake down and took his gloves off, while I made sandwiches. He asked May how she was doing. It was obvious being around other people always made her feel better.

Barkley continued to sit on May's lap. May always said she loved being over here.

I came halfway down the steps and handed her a filled plate. May jumped up and thanked me. "Oh, these are the same turkey sandwiches that I had with you before."

Chips spilled off the side of the plate, and Barkley was quick to snatch them up. I handed Paul a plate, and he sat across from me. I came back down the stairs with my plate this time and a cold beer for Paul. He deserved a beer after working so hard in the backyard.

"I'm having a Diet Coke, May, would you like one?"

She never drank diet drinks, but quietly said, "That will be fine."

The three of us enjoyed having lunch outside together. Paul had built a rock waterfall in the corner of the yard and had it going. The trickle of the water was so peaceful.

May looked around the yard and said, "I wish my backyard looked like this."

We knew May's favorite thing about our yard was the tall shrub that Paul had used his "Edward Scissorhands" skills to trim into the shape of a deer.

He had gotten a pair of antlers from his friend who hunted and placed them at the top of the deer's head as if he were looking over the fence into May's yard. We had heard those words before from May. Paul always made May feel so welcome. They could sit for hours talking about plants and gardening.

May's mind seemed clearer out here, less foggy. I knew she felt comfortable when she was around us. She told us multiple times that we were the perfect neighbors, and I knew she felt unafraid when we were with her.

I asked May in between bites, what she had been up to. May didn't want to tell us about the hellish couple of days that she'd had. She didn't want people to think she was going crazy, so she said she had been going through some old pictures.

I stopped chewing, waiting to see if she would remember anything that she had confided in me, but she went on. "I need to buy some photo albums." Which I had heard *sooooo* many times.

Paul was eager to get back to work in the yard. He thanked me for the lunch and put on his khaki-colored sun hat and his work gloves. May admired him for his hard work, and I knew that. It was important to him to have a nice-looking yard. Most people in our neighborhood took good care of theirs and always told him how nice it looked.

Paul knew when to aerate the lawn, when to fertilize the grass for which season, and what plant food to use on what plants to get them to thrive, and because of his passion and knowledge, his yard looked beautiful.

Even when Paul was tired from working in his own yard, he was always willing to help May and share his knowledge with her. I picked up the plates and carried them into the house. That should have been a cue that our lunch was over, but May didn't want to go home. She didn't want to be alone. She stayed sitting at the patio table and watched Paul trim the bushes. The sound of the trimmer was so loud that she couldn't converse with him, and I was inside doing the dishes and cleaning up.

When Paul finally turned off the trimmer to rake up the greenery that had fallen to the ground, there was music playing. I had opened up the top room window that faced the backyard and turned on an oldies radio station. I could tell that Paul enjoyed it because he started whistling along with The Mamas and the Papas.

Paul wasn't shy about singing along to the songs he knew. He had a really good voice. May seemed to enjoy sitting there and listening to him sing. I came down the redwood-colored stairs, and Barkley was right at my heels. I walked over and started scooping up the piles of shrubbery that had fallen to the ground, when Paul asked me, "Where are your gardening gloves? Those barberries are sharp; you'll get stuck with thorns."

May thought it was so nice that he was concerned about me getting pricked. I walked over to the shed and got my gloves. May continued to stay there a good part of the day, not saying much. My back started to ache, and I felt like I had had enough sun and said, "I'm going in the house and take a shower."

Paul said, "Yeah, I've about had enough too. I'm just going to put my tools away, and I'll be in as well."

Finally, May stood up to leave. She thanked us for the lunch and Diet Coke and left through the back gate. I looked out the front window as May noticed the neighbor across the street out working in the front yard. May walked over there and sat on her grass. Anything to keep from being home alone.

How sad.

It never surprised me when a new tenant moved into one of the townhomes that backed up to the park. Through the chain link fence, you could see their backyards and sometimes right through their glass sliding doors into their kitchens.

You could tell a lot from looking at their back-yards. If there were small toys, you knew it was a young family with young kids. If it had a trampoline in the backyard, you knew they had middle-grade kids. And if you saw rocking chairs, it was most likely a retired couple with potted plants around their patio.

Depending on the time of day, the mother would poke her head out to check on the little kids making sure they were okay.

Another backyard down the way had a black garbage bag spilling over with beer cans, a redwood picnic table, benches, a fire pit, and folding chairs with sports logos on them.

The yard that May liked to stop at was the yard of a Hare Krishna person's house. He had cages that had two rabbits, one brown and one black. He devoted his whole yard to the bunnies. In the middle of the yard, he had built a greenhouse. May and I watched each week that passed, to see the progress that was being made.

He brought in bales of hay, lined them up against

the fence, and placed stacks of branches that were crisscrossed in a pile, so the bunnies could nestle underneath them. People walked the path and would stop to get a look at the furry little creatures.

The dogs were well aware they were there, even if they were hiding in the sticks. One morning, I saw the guy laying on the ground. I had to do a double-take to make sure he was alive. We didn't want to disturb him in case he was sleeping, but we watched to see if we could see his chest rise and fall because he wasn't moving.

He was playing soft music, and we thought perhaps he was meditating. It was so peaceful. We felt guilty half hiding as we watched him. He suddenly stood and was practicing his sacred movements and started to chant. We couldn't understand what he was saying, and I felt like we shouldn't invade his privacy. We wondered if the well-planned backyard was providing comfort to the rabbits or privacy for his sacred times. Either way, our curiosity allowed us to snoop longer than we should have.

I whispered to May, "We'd better go."

I started to walk away and looked back, and she was still watching him. I tried to get her attention without calling out, but she wouldn't look my way. I finally walked over to her and lightly touched her on the shoulder and said, "Come on, let's go," and she finally followed me. I was glad that my dog didn't notice the bunnies and started to bark. We never knew what we were going to see at the park, both good and bad. Before May's Alzheimer's got so advanced, we talked about everything, politics, sports, family, food, and our finances. We both agreed that even though neither one of us went to a big university, we were happy with the lives we were living.

May told me the business classes she took that enabled her to have the good job she used to have. I thought about how she couldn't even work a remote control now, and how frustrating her phone was to her. I noticed now when she talked about certain family members, she couldn't remember their names anymore and would stumble around, her brain trying so hard to remember. As usual, when I could, I would fill in the blanks for her.

May never talked about having Alzheimer's, she referred to it as, "my memory problem." She realized she couldn't do things, couldn't remember things, and often told me she didn't understand why she couldn't just take the medication for memory loss she saw advertised on TV.

She was totally dependent on other people, and she hated it. Her family didn't know how long she would be able to live on her own, but they still had jobs they had to go to every day.

They knew Paul and I checked on her every single day and night. They knew how close we were with May, and it gave them some sort of peace. Her brother thanked us continuously for what we did for her. We didn't feel obligated to help her, we had grown to love her as our friend, and though she never said it, I know she loved us too.

There was a homeless man that slept in the park, all curled up in his sleeping bag. Only his messy oily hair was sticking out and a tattooed arm clutched tightly to a backpack. To the side of his arm were a water bottle and a bucket. Most of the time that we had passed him, he was asleep, but it so happened one morning that he was sitting up smoking a cigarette. As we passed him, we said good morning as we did to most people we walked past in the park.

May slowed down and walked over to the homeless man to talk to him. He asked her if she had any loose change. We never walked with money in our pockets. The whole time I'm yelling at her "come on!"

I didn't like how she stayed and talked to this man because, with her Alzheimer's, she was easily taken advantage of. When she finally could see that I was growing impatient and acted like I was going to leave her, she ran to catch up with me. When we were walking side by side, we started talking about home-less people. I told her it made me sad to see people who were experiencing homelessness.

It surprised me that she was not the least bit sym-pathetic toward them; in fact, she almost seemed irritated. She responded, "Well I didn't have anyone to help me, and I made it."

I answered back, "Well sometimes it's beyond people's control, May, we don't know what's hap-pened in their lives to cause them to have hard times. A lot of the time they have mental health issues."

But it was as if she didn't even hear a word I said. She shot back with "they're all druggies and they made the choice to take drugs."

I knew that that was not always true and made me think about how at Christmas time I would al-ways donate to the food bank, and then I would gather blankets and coats, thinking of those poor people out in the cold, and I would donate them to the homeless shelter. I would always ask May if she wanted to donate, as I knew she had a bundle of knitted scarves she had made when her memory was better. She had an abundance of blankets that I thought she could spare, but she told me no she didn't have anything to give.

It was probably the hoarder in her that made it hard for her to part with anything. Or was it that she just didn't have any compassion for those home-less people struggling to find food and a dry place to sleep only to have to leave the shelter during the day in the cold and snow in the wintertime?

I thought about how they could benefit from the warmth of those scarves. But no, they would stay in that basket at her house and not be good to anyone. Maybe it was proof that one day she was able to knit and do things on her own, and she couldn't part with them.

CHAPTER TWENTY-TWO

·······················

MY PHONE RANG, and it was my neighbor Betty that lived across the street from May.

"Marcelina, this is Betty. I thought I should let you know that Mayumi is telling people in our neighborhood that you went into her house and stole her credit card."

"What? I never stole her credit card. That makes me mad. I can't believe that she would say that about me."

"I know you wouldn't do anything like that, that's why I thought I should tell you."

I hung up and immediately told Paul what May was saying to the neighbors.

He said, "Don't worry about it, Marcelina, they know you wouldn't do anything like that."

But it really bothered me. After all, I did for her, she would turn on me. The more I thought about it, the madder I got. I was embarrassed that she was spreading untruths about me to our neighbors. I waited a couple of days and then decided to talk to her about it. When we went walking, I told her what Betty had told me, and she said, "I didn't say that."

"You did too, Betty told me. You know I wouldn't steal your credit card."

She just looked down and said, "Well, someone's coming into my house and taking things."

"Well, it's sure as hell not me. You stay away from me, and I'll stay away from you if that's what you think of me."

I cut our walk short because she acted like she didn't believe me, and that made me furious.

"That's it. I've had it," I said to Paul. I didn't go pick her up to go walking, I didn't take food over to her, I didn't take her grocery shopping, and I stayed away from her. I thought I'll show her for thinking I would do something so awful, after all I do for her. How dare she.

As it turned out, it was me who suffered. I worried about what she was doing. I hadn't seen her out. Had anyone taken her grocery shopping? Was she all right? Was she eating? I don't know why I felt like it was my responsibility to take care of her when she had family, but I did. After about two weeks, I told myself it was the disease, not her. I felt bad about all of her confusion and what it was doing to her.

I saw her go out to her mailbox, and I hurried out

the door to catch her as she stood there staring over at my house.

"May, I'm sorry, I miss you."

"I miss you too." We hugged.

I actually saw tears in her eyes. Nothing was ever said about our disagreement. I never brought the credit card issue up again, we just went back to being friends and doing what we always did, being each other's walking buddies. I wasn't sure if she even realized I had been so hurt by what she was saying about me, but I never forgot it.

May asked me if I had seen on the news there was a missing girl that was supposed to be meeting up with her friends but never showed up. It just so happened the girl had a Japanese name.

May was so distraught about it. I told her yes that I had watched the news. She was so emotional about it, that I asked her if she knew the person that was missing.

"No."

She got so caught up in the story, that every day she would ask me. "Have you heard any more about the missing girl? They showed a picture of her on the news last night."

"Yes, I saw it too."

Days later, I heard they found the girl dead. Mayumi was a mess that morning. I was sad too, but we didn't even know this person. She cried when we talked about it. The next day she asked me, "Do you know when the funeral will be?"

I wondered why she wanted to know; she didn't even know this girl. The way she was acting, you would have thought that it was her best friend.

I quickly said, "I'm not going to the funeral of somebody I don't even know."

"Well maybe my brother will take me," she said in a huff.

I wondered if she would have felt this emotional if the girl had been Caucasian. She obviously felt a connection to this person. I felt bad about the whole thing, I really did. I knew her brother wouldn't take her to the funeral of someone she didn't even know. All I could hope for was once it was not on the news anymore, she would forget all about it, and she did.

Because Mayumi and I walked so much, even in the winter, we noticed things that went on in the park. We noticed two very nice cars that were parked next to each other at the same time almost every weekday. The handsome man would get out of his Mercedes and get into a Mazda. He would kiss the lady with the long blonde hair passionately, from what we could see. She was a nice-looking woman, and he was nice-looking as well. They would sit in her car talking as we passed by. When they got out of the car, we noticed they were both dressed in business attire, as if they had left work to meet up.

They would walk around the track, he with his arm around her small waist, nuzzling each other. We wondered if they were having an affair. She would laugh and look at him lovingly, and he would lean over and kiss her again, while they strolled hand in hand.

We almost felt like we were intruding on their rendezvous. I said to May, as we rounded the corner, "I wonder how long this has been going on?"

May said, "You don't think they're married?"

"Oh, hell no, look how passionate they are with one another."

I don't think she caught on, but we giggled like schoolgirls anyway, discussing the whole scenario.

We saw an old motor home. It was tarnished with rust, had worn tires, and looked as if a bunch of hippies was camped out in the parking lot, even though there was a sign that said, No Over Night Parking, as plain as could be.

The yellowed worn blinds were always closed, so we couldn't see inside. Outside to the north of the door was a sack of empty McDonald's containers thrown on the ground. Squashed beer cans and cigarette butts were mixed in the trash.

The County Parks and Recreation workers worked so hard to take care of the park and keep it nice for the public. One county worker that we had thanked for his hard work, told us, "You wouldn't believe what we see in this park."

I could believe it because I had seen dog poop left to dry in the sun. It was sickening and it irked me that pet owners didn't have the decency or respect for others to scoop up their own dog's poop. There was even a doggie bag dispenser on the side of the brick restrooms which we never used, since the day we went in there, and a homeless man was washing in the women's restroom.

There was used toilet paper with feces at his feet. Obviously, he was cleaning himself. The stench was so strong, and the shock of seeing a man in the women's restroom was frightening.

We startled him too, and the man's red-rimmed eyes stared at us as if he were on alert to protect himself from someone. His gray wiry beard hung down his tan, wrinkled neck. He had on filthy boxer shorts, and his dirty, ragged Levi's lay in a pile on the cement floor by his brown shoes that had cardboard taped to the soles.

He stared at us, and we stared back in shock.

We immediately turned in the other direction to get out of there as fast as we could. He probably had no intention of hurting us, but the whole situation was pretty horrifying.

I wondered days afterward why he had chosen the women's bathroom instead of the men's bathroom. This was not the same man we had seen curled up in his sleeping bag that May had talked to. This man was almost wild looking and looked very threatening. We never went into the restrooms at the park ever again.

For any salesperson who came to the door, May would always take time to listen to their presentation because it was someone to talk with. Xfinity came to her door to sell her a security system with outside cameras. The more they talked to her, the more she thought she would benefit from having it, even though she already had one.

When she told me she had signed up, I said, "But May, you already have a security system."

"But this one is better."

"You don't need two. You'd better call your brother and ask him."

At times, she would get her water turned off for not paying her bill, or the power company would shut off her power. She would receive late notices, unbeknownst to her brother. A few times I would make calls for her or make online payments with her credit card. I would always remind her to put her card back in her wallet. She would be so relieved when Paul and I could help her. I finally called May's brother to tell him she needed help, and what was going on.

"My wife is in the process of taking over her bills and is going to set them up on automatic bill pay," he said. "Thanks for looking out for her."

One day she came over and I heard tap, tap, tap, on my door. When I answered it, Mayumi was in tears. She didn't get her newspaper.

"I called about it, but the lady was so rude to me."

I wasn't going to let anyone be rude to May, she was such a sweet, kind person, so I called them for her. The woman told me May didn't get her paper because there hadn't been a payment made in three months.

Then there was a time when the Girl Scouts came to May's door, and she told them, "Just order me some cookies," not knowing how to fill out the order form. She just handed over her American Express card.

I would never forget the day she came over to my house to tell me she had won the Clearing House Sweepstakes. She was so excited. She told me the person on the phone had asked her if she had been to Hawaii and used a credit card. She said, "Yes but not recently."

He said that didn't matter. That is how they got her information to call her and let her know she had won. He wanted her address because he said the news station would be there to film the whole event. She had always been told by her family not to give her information out. She told the man that she would have to let her brother know, and he told her not to wait too long or they would move down the list to someone else. After she hung up the phone, she came right over to tell me the good news. She had seen it on the television when it showed someone winning the Clearing House Sweepstakes, and she was very excited.

I asked May, "Do you even remember signing up for Clearing House?"

She looked puzzled. "I don't know."

"It may be a scam, May."

"No," she said angrily, "I won, they said so."

"I know, May, but did you give them any of your information? Did they ask for the credit card you used in Hawaii?"

"I don't know," she said.

"You better let your brother know what's happening, I'm sure he'll agree with me that it's a scam."

She looked deflated when she left my house. A couple of days later, she said she had another call from Hawaii, and she knew it was that same person calling her.

"I didn't answer the phone this time." She sounded pleased with herself. She had thought about what

Paul and I had said to her, about not giving out her information, including her address.

Her brother was mad at her for even speaking with them. She said she didn't sleep at all because she was afraid they were going to come to her house and knew that she lived alone. She told me we were right; she should have never talked to them on the phone that day.

I expressed my concerns to Paul about how vulnerable May was now. He was concerned as well.

He said, "Marcelina, we've been over this before, it's her family's decision to let her continue to live on her own, not ours."

"I know, but what are they waiting for, for hell's sake? For her to get hurt, or for someone to take advantage of her. Can't they see what she's like?"

"*No*, we see what she's like, and the care that she needs, They see her mostly on her good days."

We were sitting on the lawn in our folding chairs in the shade. It was just May and me, Paul had run to Home Depot.

Right away, May wanted to know why he had gone to Home Depot. I told her he needed to get some stepping stones for our yard. She wanted to know where we were putting them.

"I'll have Paul show you when he gets home."

I knew if he showed her, she would want him to

put them in her yard as well. After we sat there for a little while, Paul returned home and asked May if she had had her coffee this morning.

"No, I haven't, I couldn't get my coffee maker to work." Paul told her to bring it over, and he would take a look at it after he unloaded the stepping stones from the truck.

When she brought it over, the plastic reservoir for the water was missing. Paul told her to go home and get it. He explained it was impossible to make coffee without it.

She was gone a long time, and we both knew she probably couldn't find it. When she finally came back, she said almost accusingly, "It was on there when I brought it over."

Paul said, "No, May, it wasn't on there when you brought it over."

She looked at him, not sure if she believed him or not. I told them both that I would go back into our kitchen to double-check that it wasn't there.

"It's not in there, let's go over to your house, and I'll help you look for it, two sets of eyes are better than one," I said, trying to lighten things up.

We walked across her lawn to her front door. We went into her kitchen and started looking. Everything was dirty and cluttered. I started moving stuff and searching under things. I looked in the mostly bare cupboards, and I could see it was making her nervous that I had entered her zone and was invading her personal space. Food and crumbs were spilled all over the floor, and coffee had dripped down the front of the dishwasher. Her sink was filthy and stained a dark gray. I tried not to make her feel uncomfortable and looked away.

I thought of all the cleaning products that she had bought at Sam's club when we were together, and obviously never got used. Boxes of garbage bags and Ziplock bags of different sizes were stacked on top of her refrigerator, too high for her to even reach. Six-packs of soda pop were stacked on the floor as if she was having a party. The kitchen table had boxes of crackers, sacks of Cheetos, and a box of half-eaten doughnuts that appeared to be stale. The powdered sugar from the doughnuts was all over the table and had spilled on the floor. On top of the stove were dirty dish rags that smelled sour. They were covering the burners which made me feel uncomfortable, and behind them, I saw the plastic water reservoir to the Keurig.

"Here it is."

"Who put it there?" she asked. "It was on the Keurig when I brought it over to your house."

I didn't answer her, instead, I said, "Let's take this over to Paul," knowing she had a lapse of memory.

Paul put the reservoir back on and ran fresh water

through it. All kinds of coffee grounds came pouring out. Paul tried to show her how to clean it out first, but she wasn't paying attention to him.

"I'll run a K cup through it now and make you a cup of coffee."

May said, "I don't want you to use yours, I can run home and get a coffee pod."

We knew if she did that, we wouldn't see her for half an hour trying to find them, so Paul reassured her she was being silly, and we would use ours. Maybe she preferred her brand, but it didn't matter, we weren't going to let her spend the whole day searching for a dang coffee pod.

The three of us sat together talking about everything that morning. May excitedly told us that she had ordered some Japanese skin care products, over three hundred dollars worth to be exact, from her Japanese friend.

She told me her brother was mad at her for ordering that much. I thought, why would her so-called friend, knowing that Mayumi had Alzheimer's, let her order three hundred dollars worth of products she will probably not even remember she'd bought, once they were put away?

On the other hand, we tried to be so careful when we took her shopping, to try and talk her out of buying duplicate things.

Sometimes she would pick things up to put in the shopping cart, and I would say, "Now you know, May, you bought one of those last time we went shopping." I don't think she remembered, but she answered, "I know, but I want another one."

She was like a little girl in a candy store when she got out.

The weather channel had predicted monsoon winds for today. I wondered if it would be a very good idea to take May walking, but I knew how much it meant to her. We walked through the path from our neighborhood to the park. The trees overhead were bending from the wind's force, and broken branches were laying in our path. We walked around them looking up over our heads to make sure that the treetops were not going to crack off and hit us in the head.

Barkley was walking faster than normal. I assumed to get out from under the trees.

When we reached the park's walking track, the wind blew our hair exposing our foreheads and our graying roots. For a minute I thought that it was going to blow my sunglasses right off my face.

I heard a honk and looked at a gray car that was getting ready to leave. It was a couple that was friends of mine and Paul's.

They rolled their windows down and said, "It's

too windy for us to walk today, we started, but decided it wasn't worth it."

I told them that we were going to tough it out and keep going. I said goodbye and told them to keep up their walking as her husband had had some health problems, and it was good to see them out.

After they drove away, I looked at May, and she looked a little nervous about continuing on our walk until we passed the playground where there was a provider with mentally challenged kids who were enjoying themselves. It reminded me of the job I retired from, and how rewarding it was.

It was a good field for me to be in, and I really enjoyed it. They didn't care that it was windy, they were just glad to be outside. That seemed to calm May down, and we said good morning to the group. As we rounded the corner, the sound of the wind was intimidating, even to me. I thought we'll only do two laps, instead of three, and get back home out from under the threatening trees. There was going to be a free concert in the park tonight, but unless those winds calmed down, I doubted they would have a very good turnout.

I pretty much took May wherever I went these days except to my dancercise class. I liked it because you exercised to oldies music which I loved, but she said that they moved too fast for her, and she couldn't keep up. She was afraid of falling, so I went with a couple in our neighborhood I liked really well.

Paul and I would do things with them occasionally, and I knew May was jealous and felt bad that she wasn't invited, but we needed time away from her. As time went on and May's memory loss increased, I began to fill in the blanks of words she couldn't think of. When she stumbled around trying to think of the word, she would knock her head with her knuckles and say, "I am so stupid."

"No, you're not stupid, May. It's just your memory problem."

She knew a lot of the neighbors in our neighborhood, but I noticed as we walked Barkley around, she began to forget their names.

It was hard on May when Paul and I went on a sixteen-day cruise to Europe. I think she felt isolated. She missed our walking, our morning coffee time, and most of all, our conversations. She missed her connection with our dog Barkley. She grew to love him.

She would always clap her hands, and say, "Come here, bud," and he would run over and jump up on her, so she could pet him. She would lean down and rub her face on his fur.

Barkley was so used to being around May, that whenever we would mention her name, his ears would perk up, and he would bark, thinking we were going to pick her up to go walking.

May had never had a dog in her whole life. I know that she wasn't happy with us when I told her that we were going to have him stay at a kennel for sixteen days while we went on our cruise, but I'm sure she also knew that she was not capable of taking care of him for us. I think she felt like he was part her dog.

When we were on our trip, I told Paul we needed to take something home for May. She used to travel a lot before her Alzheimer's diagnosis. She used to talk about her travels and the things she had seen. She had traveled a lot more than we had.

But now she would say, "I'll never be able to travel anymore," and she would feel sad. I would try to encourage her by telling her that as long as she went with somebody who would look out for her, maybe it was possible, but May never went on another trip.

Nor could she remember the places she had gone. I could see the more time I spent with her, the more I could see how her Alzheimer's was progressing. I went over to her house like I always did to pick her up to go walking. There was no answer. I rang the doorbell again and waited thinking maybe she was downstairs rummaging through things like she sometimes did. No one came to the door, so Barkley and I left and went to the park by ourselves.

Later that Saturday afternoon about three o'clock,

I went out to get the mail because it came late today. I looked over at May's house, and she was wandering around in her front yard with her pajamas on, looking dazed.

I told her that I had come to her house to get her to go walking, and she hadn't answered her door. She said, in an almost mean tone of voice, "You did not come over to my house, I just got up."

"Mayumi, it's three o'clock in the afternoon."

She started arguing that it was morning, and I thought oh no, not again. I wasn't going to do this with her. Obviously, she didn't believe me, which was how it was starting to be all the time, so I walked away from her when she said, "You're the only one who takes me grocery shopping."

"What?" And she said it again.

"You're the only one who takes me grocery shopping."

"No, May, I know your family takes you when you need something."

I headed toward my house, and she followed me, right up to my front door, as if she were in a trance, and repeated, "You're the only one who takes me grocery shopping."

I panicked. Oh my God, why does she keep saying that? Something has to be wrong with her. Did she have a stroke?

Finally, I asked, "May, are any of your family members coming over today?"

I wasn't sure what to do. I steered her toward her house and told her to go inside and call her sister, not sure if she comprehended what I had asked her to do.

I hurried inside to call her brother. Almost out of breath, I said, "I think something's wrong with Mayumi, she keeps repeating the same thing over and over again. She is really out of it today, Yuto."

He was at work but dropped everything in a panic to come home. He said his sister had also called him and said that she was very confused and was saying something about me taking her shopping.

He took her to Insta Care where they ran some tests on her. She hadn't had a stroke. It was her Alzheimer's. I think she had gotten up early, possibly four o'clock am, which was not unusual for her, even if it was still dark outside.

Then she possibly went back to bed and got up at three o'clock in the afternoon and thought it was morning. I told Yuto she had done this before; that she gets mixed up. I didn't know what caused her to repeat what she had said over and over again. It was as if no other dialogue could penetrate her mind that day. I didn't see her for a couple of days after her episode.

She stayed in her house with her blinds closed, and I didn't bother her. It was a scary thing to watch like an alien had taken over her body. I never talked to her sister who lived up north, I only had her brother's phone number. I hated to bother him very often, only when there was a problem with May, which seemed to be more frequent now.

As usual, May would get angry if I tried to help her remember things. I watched as she struggled. It didn't do any good for me to try and help her remember. It usually made me frustrated and would make her mad at me, like she knew best.

I could tell I wasn't as patient with her as I used to be. I was growing tired of hearing the same stories over and over again. She started to wear dirty clothes. I tried to hint to her to wash her clothes, pointing out spills that were on her shirt. and all it did was make her mad at me.

The knees of her sweatpants were muddy from kneeling on the ground to weed. She didn't take care of herself anymore. She had food caked between her teeth; she needed help with her personal care.

I talked to a family member who was now coming to set up her medications. I felt bad telling her that she needed more help, but I could see that my friend was going downhill. They said that she didn't qualify for in-home care, she had too much money coming in.

She said their family is going to start coming over more.

I noticed that her brother was stopping by in the mornings before he went to work and bringing her breakfast. Paul and I continued taking dinners over to her, not every day, but when we had extra. I told a friend of mine that one night I took an enchilada casserole over to her and rang the door, and when she answered, I handed it to her, and she said, "What's this for?"

Had she forgotten all the meals in the past years that we had shared with her? So, I said, "For you to eat."

She closed the front door and didn't thank me. I don't know if she ever ate it or not. I didn't get my plate back either.

I was a person who suffered from anxiety from time to time. Mayumi provided a sense of calmness to me. Between the walking and the talking and the stories we would share with one another, she was good for me. I thought back at how she had described Japan to me, in her good days. I was enthralled listening to her talk about it. She raved about how good the Japanese food was there, saying, "you would never get Japanese food like that here."

She talked of the relatives who lived there, that spoke very little English. Her cousins were the ones who would take her around. May didn't speak Japanese, being raised in the United States, but she knew a few Japanese words and would share them with us.

When something tasted good, she would say "Oishi," meaning delicious or good tasting. Mayumi told me how she loved to go shopping in Tokyo at the Giza shopping center. She said it was a shopper's haven, even though it was expensive.

She would buy name-brand purses, T-shirts, and glassware, and she would pay to have them shipped home. She didn't care, she was having the time of her life. She loved it there.

She told me her family had tickets to attend a sumo wrestling match and how interesting it was, but she said she wouldn't go to another one. The Imperial Palace was one of her favorite things to see. She explained that it was still in use by the Imperial family, and they weren't allowed inside, but she said the East Gardens were beautiful.

She described how at a distance you could see Mt. Fiji. Her cousin took them to the Kabuki-za Theater to watch performances. I could tell as she described things that it was the shopping and the food that excited her the most. She told me she always brought an empty suitcase along for her shopping sprees.

There was one particular restaurant, where the hostesses wore kimonos, and it had a tempura counter. She loved eating there, but there was a time that her sister went with her, and she told her she didn't like Japanese food, and she didn't see why they had to have it for every meal.

After all, she said, "They're Americanized now."

It caused feelings among the cousins, and Mayumi was embarrassed by it, saying she was never going to invite her sister to go to Japan with her again. I asked her, "Would you ever want to live in Japan with your cousins?"

"I couldn't afford to. It's so expensive there. I'm just thankful I can vacation there as often as I can."

As time went on, I heard the same story of her going to Japan and how she would never invite her sister ever again, not remembering she had told me several times before. I just listened to her repeat her memory of Japan because I knew it made her happy. If I ever reminded her that she already told me something, she would just ignore me and go on telling me the same thing anyway, as if I wasn't even there, and she was talking to someone else.

Sometimes I could see the fog come over her as if she was far away. She would have that blank look that she would get. I was glad I was with her most of those times, afraid to leave her alone. Since I spent so much time with her, I recognized the changes. She was getting confrontational and stubborn. Even a small thing like me telling her she had her shirt on backward could make her angry, and then later in the day, she would have completely forgotten about it.

One night we called her to tell her we were going to pick up a chicken salad and asked her if she wanted us to pick one up for her. She always seemed so thankful when we included her, and it made me feel better knowing she was eating, which could be hit and miss now, depending on how she was doing that day.

I noticed one night when I took the dog out to go potty in the middle of the night that May's lights were still on at two o'clock in the morning. She had started staying up all night. She told me that she sometimes talks to her dead mother.

I looked at her face and replied, "If it makes you feel good, that's okay."

She looked relieved that I didn't think she was crazy. She was really worried about going crazy because of the devastating things she was experiencing and didn't understand. I wished I could go to her doctor's appointment to see how they were explaining to her what was happening, but I knew it was out of the question, even though I felt like I was family, I really wasn't.

CHAPTER TWENTY-THREE

....

ONE DAY I was in the bathroom putting my makeup on, and Paul was talking to me from the kitchen when we heard the back door close.

He stopped talking and said he had thought well for rude; I was talking to Marcelina, and she leaves and goes out the back door.

When Paul walked over to the hall, there stood Mayumi.

It caught him off guard to see her in our house, and he later said it scared him to death. "Mayumi, what are you doing here, this is my house."

She looked disoriented and yelled, "No, this is my house."

I came out of the bathroom to see what was going on and saw her standing in our hall and how troubled she looked.

Calmly, I said, "May, come in and sit down and visit with us."

She spat back, "No, this is my house, get out."

As she was pulling away from Paul, he opened the back door leading to the garage, and said, "See, there's Marcelina's car."

But she shouted, "No, that's my car." She didn't notice Paul's white truck was parked next to my car. Paul led her down our back steps and went out front, pointing to her house, and said, "There, that's your house."

She still kept turning around, looking at the front of our house as if she was unsure. Next thing he knew, he heard her door slam hard and loud, as if she was irritated at him.

When Paul came in, he said, "That was weird, she thought this was her house."

We didn't see her for days and never mentioned the incident to anyone.

It had been two weeks, and I was sitting on my couch with Barkley and my son's dog, Bossco.

I could see Paul mowing the back lawn through the sliding glass door. I always loved the smell of freshly cut grass but decided to close it because of the noisy lawnmower.

I went on reading my book and playing with the dogs when all of a sudden I could hear yelling. I looked up and saw May attacking Paul.

Blood was running down his arm.

She was yelling, "Get out of here! Get out of here!" She was screaming and acting like a wild animal.

I jumped up off the couch and went to open the door to see what I could do, but when I started to come out to help Paul, he frantically yelled, "Go back in the house and lock the door. Call 911. I can't control her."

I watched in horror as he tried to hold her at bay, but she kept coming at him, sinking her claws into his flesh, and screaming, "You stole my lawnmower, get out."

Paul tried to tell her, "May, you're in my yard, this is my lawnmower."

But no amount of reasoning would work.

I called 911 dispatch and told them that our neighbor with Alzheimer's was attacking my husband and to hurry because he had blood running down his arm.

At that point, I looked out again, and she was leaning down to bite him. My whole body started to shake in fear. My heart was pounding hard, and I wanted to help Paul, but he was trying to protect me, thinking that she might attack me next. He went around the patio table to get away from her, and she started to throw things. Ceramic vases with plants crashed to the ground. A statue of a Mexican man with a sombrero from our Mexico trip, went flying, almost hitting Paul, and broke into little pieces on the cement.

I couldn't believe my eyes as she chased him around the table trying to claw at him. Such anger and hate seemed to perpetuate her adrenaline to fight.

Paul said later that he didn't want to hurt her, after all, she was our friend, so he took it and didn't fight back.

He just tried to push her away when she came at him.

She stumbled and fell into the flower bed, but immediately jumped up and went at him again.

I went to look out the front window to see if the police were here yet. The dogs were barking sensing something was wrong. Everything was out of control.

Then May must have spotted the shovel leaning up against the shed. When Paul leaned over to pick up a broken pot, she whacked him across the back with the shovel with all of her might.

He fell to the ground, unable to breathe.

I opened up the door and screamed, "OH MY GOD! MAY GO HOME!"

She didn't even look up at me. The neighbors next door heard all of the commotion and came running through the side gate where May had sneaked in. They saw what had happened. Paul was laying on the ground out of breath and shocked at what she had done to him. With help from the neighbor, he was able to shakily stand up holding on to his back in pain.

"Look what she did to me!" His arm was a bloody mess from his wrist to his upper arm, and bruises were starting to form. The neighbor walked May out into the front yard.

There was no expression on May's face. She stared ahead, her eyes blank, lost.

Our neighbor put her arms around May and hugged her tightly as she continually talked softly in her ear. I didn't know what she said, but it seemed to calm May down.

She didn't even seem to notice what she had done to Paul.

Suddenly, May broke out of the embrace, walked across the street, and tried to get into that house, but the door was locked.

We all watched in shock, wondering what she was going to do next. She was so confused.

Just then two police cars drove up in front of our house. One policeman hurried over to Paul to see if he needed medical attention, and the other policeman went over to take Mayumi back to her house.

She pointed at Paul and screamed, "There he is, see?"

Obviously she really believed he had done something wrong.

Paul relayed that May had come through the unlocked gate to the backyard while he was mowing and grabbed onto him, yelling, "You stole my lawnmower."

The policeman was worried about Paul's back and said he could call for an ambulance to come, but Paul wouldn't let him. He wanted to get his story out of what had happened. He was shaking and I was too.

The policeman asked, "Do you want to press assault charges against her?"

"Oh no," we both said in unison.

We told him how long we had been neighbors, and that we were best friends with May.

"I can't understand why she would do this to me?" Paul sighed.

Paul called May's brother and told him what had happened, and he said he would come right over. We know now without a shadow of a doubt, that if there had been a rake leaning up against the shed, rather than a shovel, in May's beastly rage, she would have stabbed him with the rake and could have killed him.

The second policeman guided May home and took her into her house, so she couldn't see us and get more agitated.

They waited for her brother to come. In the end, four police cars showed up. When we were finished telling our side of the story and they made sure Paul was going to be all right, they left.

We came into our house, and Paul had a beer to settle his rattled nerves. We talked about what a weird ordeal we had just been through and felt traumatized by the whole thing.

Paul said that he hoped May's brother would come over and talk to us so that he could tell him everything that happened, and how out of control she had been.

I told him, "He'll come over and talk to us, honey, he's a good person."

Paul went in to take a shower and clean the blood off his arm. The doorbell rang, and it was our neighbor Betty, who lived across the street from May. She wanted to see if Paul was okay.

I invited her in and showed her the pictures of Paul's bloody arm I had taken with my cell phone.

She shrieked in horror, "She did that to him?"

"Yes, and he wouldn't let me come out to help him."

"Oh my God!" she said.

Just as I was telling her about the attack, the doorbell rang again. This time it was May's brother, Yuto.

I invited him in to sit down and told him that Paul was in the shower and that I would go tell him that he was here.

Our neighbor Betty said, "I'm going to go home, and let you guys talk. I'll call you tomorrow, Marcelina."

She hugged me and said, "Let me know if you guys need anything," and left.

Paul came into the family room with his hair still wet from the shower. The lacerations and bruises were apparent, even though the blood had been washed off. His back was black and blue, and he could hardly stand upright, he was in so much pain.

Paul softly shook Yuto's hand and slowly lowered himself into his easy chair. Yuto said, "I wanted to come over and say how sorry I am about this whole thing, you guys have been so good to her."

I had sent him the gruesome pictures of Paul's arm that I had taken. He told us that the policeman said someone needed to be with Mayumi around the clock if she was going to continue living there.

I told Yuto, "May told us that her previous employer had given her a gun with a pearl handle."

"We're worried about her state of mind and owning a gun," said Paul.

I sadly told him, "I don't feel safe living next door to her anymore, and that breaks my heart to say."

My chin started to quiver, and I started to cry.

Paul said, "I can't believe this even happened."

I added, "We love her, that was not our Mayumi out there."

Her brother looked down. "I know, it's the disease," he said sadly.

I cried even harder as we recited the good times we had with May. We were both emotionally distraught. It was very traumatizing.

"We just couldn't understand why she would attack Paul for no reason."

Yuto shook his head. "I don't know either. I'm so sorry," he said one last time. We hugged him, and he left, saying he needed to get back to her.

Her brother did what the police told him to do. He stayed overnight with May, and then her sister would come during the day until he got off work.

Yuto told us with obvious regret, "I knew that the day would come when we would have to put Mayumi into a memory care facility, but I didn't think it would be so soon." They couldn't take the chance of her attacking anyone else.

Paul wanted to take a nap; he was worn out after what had happened. He stretched his easy chair out to where he could lay back and relieve some of the pain he was experiencing. I had given him some pain medication and hoped that it would kick in. I laid my head back on the couch and closed my eyes, but my mind would not shut down.

I couldn't get the picture of May attacking Paul out of my head, and the aggression that empowered her. I knew I wasn't going to be able to nap, so I quietly, as to not wake Paul, went into our computer room and started to search online about Alzheimer's disease.

I wanted to learn more about this dreaded condition, and I read how individuals experiencing Alzheimer's may not seem like his or herself. It said some people with AD may express irritability or even outright aggression toward others, especially loved ones.

Yup, I thought, that was May.

It went on to say that the disturbing behaviors typically stem from their feeling fatigued, overwhelmed, or frustrated. Physical outbursts are symptoms of the disease and must not be taken personally.

Oh my gosh, I was so glad I had read that. I read it again, physical outbursts are symptoms of the disease and must not be taken personally.

I needed Paul to read this when he's up from his nap. We must not take it personally. I went on reading. The article talked about the affected person accusing family members of stealing their belongings when apparently, they were misplaced.

It talked about paranoia and how the disease victim believes that everyone around wants to cause them harm. They sometimes suffer from hallucinations, hearing nonexistent voices. Seeing objects which are not present. They experience high tension, irritability, and amplified anxiety. There it was in a nutshell. That described May to a "T."

What I really wanted to know was, had there ever been a case where a person with dementia or Alzheimer's ever killed someone? I found an article in the *New York Times*. There was a man who was living at a senior living complex who had killed his friend that lived there. He had put a plastic bag over her head and suffocated her. The residents and staff were shocked because they had walked together, eaten their meals together, and at times he would sweetly read to her.

He didn't understand what made him kill her, but he admitted he did it. The staff didn't think he would be charged because of him having dementia, but he was charged with first-degree murder. He went to jail for a year and was transferred to a state hospital for the criminally insane for about two years.

Finally, the charges were dropped. They moved him to a different living facility, where they could ensure the safety of everyone, including himself.

He spent nearly three years in the criminal justice system, and it was very hard on him. It went on to say, he deteriorated quickly and was scared all the time. He would walk back and forth talking to himself. He would cry and be very confused. It was such a sad article that upset me, but I went on to read more.

That man had never been violent in his whole life. The article went on to tell of more cases where someone was killed by a person with Alzheimer's.

I stopped. I couldn't read anymore. My heart was breaking, thinking of what could have happened. I talked with friends who had parents with the disease, but none of their loved ones experienced violence.

They said they were *belligerent,* but not violent. I could do all the research I could, but nothing would tell us what on that day would have made May come into our backyard and attack Paul. It was an ongoing problem for the police. There are cases where the police were called to a domestic disturbance, often in homes of couples who had been happily married for many years, and the police might not realize the belligerent spouse has dementia.

I thought how lucky we had been because when I made the 911 call to the police, I had told them it was our neighbor who had Alzheimer's, so they had a little heads up about what they were going to be dealing with. The article went on to say throwing individuals with dementia in jail is inhumane. I was glad we hadn't pressed charges against Mayumi nor was it ever considered.

When I woke up that morning, the first thing I thought was, today was the day that May's family was going to place her in a memory care facility. I felt sorry for May's brother Yuto, as I knew his heart was breaking having to do this. I had asked him a couple of days ago if he had told her she was going to a facility, and he said, "No, the family is trying to decide how to get her there."

His face was so sad as he explained the pressure he was feeling having to take his sister out of her home. He said the family was devastated.

This was not going to be an easy thing. May would tell me she was never going to leave her house; she always she said would die there.

I didn't want to be home today. I felt sad knowing what was going to take place. I knew how May was going to fall to pieces when she found out they were taking her away from her home she vowed to never leave.

Paul and I decided we would take our dog and go to the farmer's market for the day, to get away. Later that night when we came home, all of May's family's cars were parked outside her house. The front door was propped open, and her bed and mattress were out on the lawn. Immediately, I could feel the sadness envelop me.

The tears were forming in my eyes. I wanted to hurry into the house, shut the blinds, and not think about what was happening to my friend. I felt sick to my stomach, thinking she was inside there crying, watching them haul her furniture, her life, out the front door. My good friend who we shared so many good times, who was like family to us, would be gone.

I think Paul and I felt guilty about May being taken out of her home. What if we hadn't called the police that day? What if Paul had fought her off? Would he have hurt her? But she was out of control. She had injured Paul. She had been so out of it with rage, that we felt that Paul needed help with her.

Months later, May's brother told us that she had attacked two more people at the memory care facility. She said that they were making fun of her. They took her to a psychiatric hospital to evaluate her. May's brother was concerned they wouldn't let her go back to the facility where she was living, and he would have to look for another care center to place her.

Weeks later, he let us know that he was able to get her back in, and he was relieved. He told us about how she would cry to come home, saying she could take care of herself. How often would those outbursts of anger and confusion happen, if he were to agree to let her come home?

It was not possible. I'm sure he remembered me saying, "I don't feel safe with her living there any-more" after the attack. I felt guilty saying that about my best friend, but it was like an entity had taken over her body, and we were her enemies. The transformation of her facial expressions was completely different from the person we knew. Fear and hatred had replaced that soft, tan, smiley face we had grown accustomed to.

I asked about May whenever her brother was at her house taking more items out or picking up the mail. Yuto shared with us that it had taken three people to settle her down when they first took her there. She was kicking and screaming the whole way. But the issue was, she could not take care of herself and be safe, and safety was the main issue.

He told me, "She keeps trying to get out the doors, but she's not able to because you need a code."

Yuto continued, "She told me she was going to walk home."

I finally asked if we could go visit her, and he slowly said, "She still blames you guys for coming into her house and stealing things from her. If our family members try to tell her any different, that you didn't, she gets angry."

In her mind that was the way it was. Neighbors who cared for her, did for her, were now bad in her mind. It hurt us deeply that our good friend would never be like she was before. She wouldn't remember the good times we had, and how close we three were, but we would never forget her.

CHAPTER TWENTY-FOUR

············

*O*T HAD BEEN TWO YEARS since the incident happened between May and Paul. I received a phone call from my old boss where I used to work. She wanted to meet for breakfast and catch up on what both of us had been doing.

I was glad that she called and was looking forward to getting together with her. She knew about what had gone on with our neighbor because she and I had a long phone conversation right after it happened. I told her about the emotional trauma that we had been put through and how devastated we were.

We met at a restaurant near both our houses. When she got out of her car, I was standing in front of the restaurant doors. She walked right toward me and threw her arms around me. "It's been way too long since we've seen each other."

I hugged her back. After we were seated and had our coffee served, the first thing she said was, "How's Paul doing?"

"He suffers with pretty severe pain now. He's been going to physical therapy for months. I bought him a massager for his chair, which rolls up and down his back and has heat. It gives him some relief, but I don't think he will ever be the same."

"Do you still walk?"

I told her I try to, but I miss my walking buddy. "Other ladies in our neighborhood have offered to walk with me, but I just can't do it. I missed her so much."

I tried not to cry.

She reached into her handbag and brought out a small pocketbook, wrapped in a flour sack dish towel she had embroidered.

The small book was titled *How To Walk* by Thich Nhat Hanh, a book about mindfulness. As I read through it, the sayings resonated with me. To appreciate feeling the earth beneath my feet and appreciate that I can walk. I always filled my mind with thoughts and memories as I walked, especially now.

The book said to absorb the sights around me. I could feel my lungs working as I breathed in and breathed out. It was a form of walking meditation the handbook had talked about. It was so exhilarating for me, just what I needed to encourage me to keep going.

Today at the store, I saw a bonsai tree. It reminded me of Mayumi, and how she told me once that she was going to take a bonsai class. I remembered how I told her that I didn't have the tolerance to trim them and keep them healthy and alive.

I was so tempted to buy it and take it over to the care center. We knew where it was located because we passed it on our way when taking our granddaughters to school.

I thought of what Yuto said to us about her still being angry, and I decided against it. She would probably go ballistic if she saw Paul and me and would probably throw it at us. I couldn't take it home because it would just make me sad thinking she never got to take her class.

Our granddaughter is now living in our downstairs apartment while she goes to college. I'm actually glad that Mayumi is gone now so that I don't have to worry about our granddaughter leaving the garage door open, and Mayumi coming up our back stairs into our house thinking it was hers.

Today there is a breeze blowing as I walk the pathway to the park. My feet kick up dirt that's smashed to the ground. Trees line both sides of the path welcoming all who want entry to the park. There's a large stump from a tree that was cut down. It sometimes resembles a man hunched over.

To the left of the trees is the dry canal that runs the whole length of the path. On the other side of the canal is an older white house with a large yard. There was a sign that said, Private Property, Keep Out.

There was that same man May and I would always see, we called him "the keeper of the path."

He was a pleasant man. If we said good morning, he would always stop what he was doing to talk about the weather. He was retired now he said, and his brother who lived with him had a stroke and was now in a rehabilitation facility. He stood tall in his Levi's and flannel shirt, with his shovel shoved halfway into the dirt. He leaned on the handle as he talked.

He needed a shave, and his salt and pepper hair was disheveled. I could see why the high school kids who passed through the path or hid in the trees, would be scared of him. He had every right to be cross with the kids leaving their garbage on the path or tossing it into the canal.

I always wondered what kind of stories the kids concocted about the "scary old man" who lived next to the canal, especially at night.

He asked me where my friend was, and I told him she had to be put in a memory care facility. That led him to tell me about his wife who had cancer, and how he took care of her until her dying day. We both had our sad stories to tell. I told him I had better get going before I changed my mind about walking because I didn't feel very motivated these days.

It was fall now, and when I entered the park, it felt so different. It was almost empty of people since school was back in session. The old beaten-down motor home with the hippies was gone, as was the couple who would meet there for their rendezvous.

The usual small group of high school kids skipping school were there on the swings. A couple of them appeared to be asleep on the lawn.

I felt a little concerned walking by myself. I missed my comrade. I wish I could go visit her. Every day that goes by I miss her. I am surprised at how her absence in my life has left me empty and full of memories that we will never share again. Why is it I feel so devastated that May was put in an assisted living center when my own sister was just placed in one two weeks ago?

I was excited for her to get the care she needed. It was a beautiful place. She was happy to go there. Maybe it was because I could go see my sister any time I wanted, but with May with her mental condition, I knew I would never see her again.

As I walked past her dark house, I realize it's just an empty shell now. No sports programs on the television, no sweets lining her kitchen table, and no origami lined up along the fireplace mantel. Just plants wilting like Mayumi was. How long she would live on, was anybody's guess. Winter will be coming, and then I won't need excuses anymore for not walking. The bitter cold will keep me inside, only going out for necessities.

Paul will continue to clear the snow off Mayumi's driveway and sidewalks as her family comes by little by little to dispose of things that are of no importance to them.

Parts of Mayumi's broken life still lay in disarray in her house, chipped away like her memory. Piles of filled garbage sacks are stacked high for the garbage man to pick up every week. I thought about how May told me that when she dies, she knew her nieces wouldn't care about the Japanese things she had acquired in her lifetime. She said they wouldn't want any of her stuff, like the Japanese fabric which was her mother's.

She always said that her sister didn't know she had the fabric squares that her mother quilted together. She didn't show them to her because she didn't want her sister to have them, even though her sister was a really good seamstress. I was always surprised that she wouldn't share them with her since she couldn't remember how to sew any longer.

The first thing I thought when I saw her sister loading things into her vehicle was, there goes the fabric with the little Asian girls on it with colorful umbrellas. Hopefully, now, it would get made into a blanket. What a shame it was to have it stuffed in sacks and boxes that would never find purpose until now. I'm sure that Mayumi's family would find unused gift cards that were probably stashed in the bottom of an old purse somewhere.

Yuto had told me that they had found money stashed under her mattress. Who knows what else they would find week to week, month to month?

CHAPTER TWENTY-FIVE

．．．．．．．．．．．．．．．．．．．．．．．．

*T*HIS WEEK is the last week we would take our trailer out. We wondered at times if we should sell it and start staying in hotels or rent a condo when we traveled.

It was a lot of work, mainly for Paul. He has a bad back now because of Mayumi hitting him with the shovel. It had taken a toll on his whole body. I knew how strenuous it could be on him.

It was fall, and it was fun to see the leaves changing colors on the trees as we drove to our campsite. The freeway we took was so busy now with long-haul rigs driving as fast as they dared to make their destination.

They made our truck tremble as they whizzed by us.

I wondered if Paul was getting too old to haul a trailer anymore. He complained about the traffic, and how damn fast everybody went nowadays. But I knew how much he enjoyed it once we got there and he got things set up.

He would sit in his folding chair and look out in the distance to where we had seen deer on the mountainside. Trees shaded the area where we were camped, and it felt nice.

On this nice autumn day, I couldn't help but think of the disastrous camping trip when we took Mayumi with us.

I thought I'm not ready to give this up yet. This particular RV resort had become my favorite campground. The owners kept it in such good shape, and the staff was so friendly, always willing to accommodate us. We didn't need anybody else to keep us company.

Paul and I had been married for so long that our thoughts were always on the same wavelength. We enjoyed the same things, and we appreciated the solitude. We still loved each other and appreciated our time together, being thankful to have companionship at this time of our lives.

Our four days of camping went by fast. We got a lot of walking in, but I was glad to get back home. We would start our fall cleanup now that we were back. Paul backed our trailer into the tight spot next to Mayumi's house. It sits empty now. Void of any life. We never understood why the ones who did so much for her and loved her like family, she would turn against us so fiercely. It hurt us terribly, and if I thought about it long enough, I would still cry after all this time.

To have someone say things about you that are not true is so very hurtful. Paul and I never went into Mayumi's house without her, nor did I steal her credit card or anything else of hers. Paul certainly did not steal her lawnmower, and everyone knew it but her.

She was such a big part of my life that I couldn't forget her. As tears formed in my eyes, I thought that maybe someday, they would sell her house, and hopefully, a nice young family would move next door bringing happiness and light to that home.

Paul is taking Spanish classes now, and I am doing volunteer work, working with children with special needs. We decided, without much hesitation, to book a trip to Japan. We are going to enjoy all the sights and memories Mayumi no longer remembers.

I lost my friend, one word at a time.

THE END

AUTHOR'S NOTE

Dear Reader,

I do not pretend to know all there is to know about Alzheimer's disease and how it can affect each person differently. This is a work of fiction. Any references to real people and places are fictitious.

What I do want to endorse is the love, patience and understanding the person with the disease deserves and needs. The caregivers bless their hearts, should be given love, respect and support, someone to listen to their needs as well.

With the permission of the Alzheimer's Association, I have listed some resources that I hope might be helpful.

With love and compassion,

Debbie Stark

Alzheimer's Association • www.alz.org

Alzheimer's Association of Utah
124894 S. Pony Express Road, Suite 300, Draper, UT 84020
801-265-1944

24/7 HELPLINE 1800.272.3900
Home office: 225 N. Michigan Ave. Floor 17 Chicago, IL 60601

ACKNOWLEDGMENTS

FIRST AND FOREMOST, thank you to my husband Larry, who supported and collaborated with me to write this book that was so important to me to write. Thank you to my editor Debbie Ilher Rassmussen for being with me every step of the way, directing me and guiding me with her knowledge to the end. Thank you for your patience—I couldn't have done it without you! Thank you to Kim Autry for proof reading my book to make it the best that it could be. Thank you to Ashley Cannuli for my book cover design and the wonderful work that she provided.

Thank you to Francine Platt for her exquisite formatting for my books interior design. It made my book come alive and warmed my heart.

Thank you to my early on beta readers and friends, Paula Enquist, Anneke Enquist, Vicki Pedler, my daughter Shelbie Watson, Mike and Jinny Shell, Pat Iverson, Christine Amo, Marsha Nichols and Christine Nguyen. Thank you for encouraging me to move forward with it.

Much love, Debbie

ABOUT THE AUTHOR

....

DEBBIE STARK worked for The Division of Services for People with Disabilities for over 18 years. She studied Spanish for two and a half years.

Born and raised in Utah, she continues to live there with her husband of forty-nine years. She has two children and seven grandchildren.

Debbie likes to walk, read and enjoys listening to music, and as of late writing. She decided to write this story about two friends because she had a friend that was diagnosed with Alzheimer's disease. Though this is not her friends story, she couldn't help but think about what their friendship was like before she lost her to Alzheimer's.

Debbie's love for writing has encouraged her to keep writing. She has started a second novel. She will keep you updated on it's progress and hope that you found *The Pathway to Friendship – What She Didn't Remember* interesting and informative.

www.authordebbiestark.com

9 781958 626221